AZIYADÉ

AZIYADÉ

Pierre Loti

Translated by Marjorie Laurie

KEGAN PAUL INTERNATIONAL
LONDON AND NEW YORK

First published in 1927 by T. Werner Laurie Ltd
This edition published in 1989 by Kegan Paul International Limited
PO Box 256, London WC1B 3SW

Distributed by
International Thomson Publishing Services Ltd
North Way, Andover, Hants SP10 5BE
England

Routledge, Chapman and Hall Inc
29 West 35th Street
New York, NY 10001, USA

The Canterbury Press Pty Ltd
Unit 2, 71 Rushdale Street
Scoresby, Victoria 3179
Australia

Printed in Great Britain by
T. J. Press (Padstow) Ltd,
Padstow, Cornwall

ISBN 0 7103 0316 5

PREFACE

BY PLUNKETT, FRIEND OF LOTI.

A description of the hero is indispensable to a well-constructed romance. This book, however, is not a romance, or, at least, it is one that is as devoid of all plan as was the life of its hero. 'Tis, moreover, no easy task to present to an indifferent public a portrait of the Loti whom we loved. The ablest pen might well go astray in the attempt.

For Loti's physical presentment, dear reader, consult Musset. In Namouna, an Oriental tale, you may read :

" Well-set, well groomed . . . .
  Patrician hands, proud port, and nimble frame,
  Eyes that would set a woman's heart aflame."

Like Hassan, he was of a joyous temperament, but could be very sullen; he was childishly unsophisticated, but could be incredibly bored. In good as in evil, he always went the full distance; but we were fonder of him than of that egoist Hassan, and perhaps it is Rolla to whom Loti should rather be compared.

" Ofttimes in one soul two sides you shall mark.
  Above are waters that reflect heaven's blue,
  Beneath is slime, sad, hideous, stagnant, dark."

PLUNKETT.

AZIYADÉ

I

SALONICA

LOTI'S DIARY

I

May 16th, 1876.

A lovely day in May. Bright sun and cloudless sky. The foreign boats drew alongside just as the executioners on the wharf were putting the finishing touches to their work. In the presence of a crowd, six victims were writhing in the horrible last contortions of hanging. Windows and roofs were packed with spectators, while from a neighbouring balcony the Turkish functionaries smilingly contemplated a scene that had for them no novelty. The Sultan's Government had gone to no unnecessary expense in erecting the apparatus of punishment. The gibbets were so low that the bare feet of the malefactors touched the ground, their toenails scratching the sand convulsively.

II

The execution over, the soldiers withdrew, leaving the dead bodies exposed to public view till nightfall. All that day, standing erect on their feet, the six corpses grinned up at the glorious Turkish sun, with the hideous grimace of death, while callous wayfarers passed them by and young women stood around in silent groups.

III

The French and German Governments had demanded these simultaneous executions, as a reprisal for that massacre of Consuls, which had shocked Europe in the early stages of the crisis in the Near East. All the European Powers had despatched their grim ironclads into the Salonica roadstead. England was one of the first to demonstrate. That was how I came to Salonica aboard one of Her Majesty's corvettes.

IV

About four o'clock one fine spring afternoon I happened to halt by the closed door of an old mosque to watch two storks fighting. It was not long since the massacres, three bare days since the executions, and leave to go on shore had only recently been granted. The scene was a street in the old Mussulman quarter. Tumbledown houses stood on either side of narrow winding alleys, which were overhung to half their breadth by *shaknisirs,* a kind of balcony, shuttered and barred, used as a private outlook post, with tiny invisible peepholes for spying upon the passers-by. Tufts of wild oats were springing up between the dark cobble-stones and fresh green branches waved above the housetops. I caught glimpses of clear blue sky, and the balmy air of May pervaded every corner. The population of Salonica still manifested towards us a constrained and hostile attitude, while we had orders to drag our swords and a whole panoply of war through the streets. Here and there a turbaned form would slip past, hugging the wall. Not a single woman showed her head behind the protecting bars of the *haremliks.* It seemed a city of the dead.

I had supposed myself so utterly alone, that I was strangely moved on noticing close to me, at the level of my head, behind thick bars of iron, a pair of great green eyes intent upon my own. The eyebrows were brown and met in a slight frown. Courage and candour were mingled in that glance, which was like a child's, all innocence and youth.

The lady of the eyes rose and showed herself down to the girdle, in the long stiff folds of a Turkish *fereje* (mantle) of green silk embroidered in silver. A white veil was arranged with care over her head, revealing only her forehead and her enormous eyes. The irises were of a vivid emerald, that sea-green hue celebrated by the Eastern poets of old.

That is how I first saw Aziyadé.

V

Aziyadé gazed at me fixedly. She would have hidden herself from a Turk. But a giaour hardly counts as a man. At the most he is a curiosity to be examined at leisure. She was evidently surprised to find that one of those foreigners, who had come to intimidate her country with those grim iron monsters, was a mere stripling, whose appearance inspired neither terror nor disgust.

VI

I returned to the quay to find that all the ships' boats had left. Those green eyes had fascinated me mildly, although I could only guess at the lovely face beneath the white veil. Three times I had walked past the mosque on which the storks were fighting, and the afternoon had slipped away unheeded.

Every conceivable obstacle lay between this fair creature and myself: the impossibility of our interchanging a single thought, of my writing or speaking to her; the order forbidding us to be absent from our ships after six in the evening, or ever to go ashore unarmed;

our probable and final departure within a week, and, to crown everything, the jealous supervision always exercised over the harems.

I watched the last English boats drawing further and further away. I watched the sun sinking below the horizon. Then, irresolute, I sat down under the awning of a Turkish café.

VII

I was at once surrounded by a rabble of those boatmen and porters, who haunt the quays of Salonica and live under the open sky. They wanted to know why I had remained on shore, and waited there in the hope that I might require their services.

Among these Macedonians I noticed a man with one of those quaint beards, one mass of separate little curls, such as you see in the earliest statues of the country. He was sitting on the ground at my feet and was examining me with great curiosity. My clothes, and my boots in particular, seemed to interest him vastly. He stretched himself with the winning airs and graces of a big Angora cat, and when he yawned he displayed two rows of tiny, pearl-like teeth. He had a very fine head and gentle eyes, bright with intelligence and honesty. He was ragged and barelegged and his shirt was in tatters, but he was as clean as a cat.

This personage was Samuel.

VIII

How surprised I should have been, had anyone told me that these two, this man and this woman, whom I met the self-same day, were soon to play a part in my own existence, and for the space of three months to risk their lives on my account. Subsequently, both were to leave their country to follow me, and we were destined to spend the winter together under one roof, at Stamboul.

IX

Samuel mustered courage to fire off at me his half dozen words of English.

"Do you want to go on board? *Te portarem col la mia barca*," he continued in Sabir.

Samuel, it seemed, knew Sabir. It struck me at once how useful a plucky, intelligent lad, who spoke a language common to both of us, might prove on that wild adventure, which, vaguely conceived, was already hovering before my eyes.

I could no doubt buy the allegiance of this ragamuffin, but money was scarce with me. And then Samuel seemed too respectable a fellow to act, for the sake of money, the part of go-between.

X

To William Brown, lieutenant in the 3rd Regiment of Infantry, quartered in London.

————

Salonica, June 2nd.

. . . At first it was only a fever of the senses and the imagination. Then, to my surprise and delight, a new element crept in—love, or something very like it. Could you have followed your friend Loti to-day through the streets of an old and little frequented quarter of the town, you would have seen him climbing the steps of an out-landish-looking house, whose door closes mysteriously behind him. He finds this hut convenient when he wishes to assume one of those histrionic disguises in which he delights. Once you remember it was for the bright eyes of Isabel B——, the operatic star. My changing room then was sometimes a four-wheeler, sometimes a house in Haymarket, where the magnificent Martyn kept his mistress. Such an old game is this business of dressing up, that even the Oriental costume can hardly lend it the faintest charm of novelty.

Opening scene of the melodrama: A dark old room with no indications of wealth, but abundance of Oriental colour. Narghilehs and weapons lie strewn about the floor.

Behold your friend Loti in the middle of the room with three old Jewesses silently busying themselves about him. They have hooked noses and are picturesquely garbed in flowing, spangled tunics, with necklaces of threaded sequins, and catogans of green silk. Swiftly they divest him of his uniform and set to work to array him in Turkish dress, beginning with the garters and gilded gaiters, which they kneel down to adjust. Loti preserves the brooding and sombre demeanour befitting a hero of melodrama. Two or three daggers, with silver, coral-studded handles and blades damascened with gold, are thrust into his belt. A gold-embroidered tunic with flowing sleeves is slipped over his head, and a tarboosh adds the finishing touch. The old dames express their admiration by gestures and run off to fetch a large mirror.

Loti is not altogether displeased with his reflection. He smiles sadly at himself in this disguise, which may cost him his life. Then he slips out through a back door and makes his way through a whole, grotesque, pre-posterous city of mosques and Eastern bazaars. Un-heeded he glides through motley throngs, gay with all the brilliant colours affected by the Turks. Now and then, perhaps, a white-veiled woman murmurs as he passes:

"There goes a well-dressed Albanian, with beautiful weapons."

Prudence forbids you, my dear William, to proceed further in your friend's footsteps. At his journey's end there awaits him an amourette with a Turkish lady, who is wife to a Turkish husband—an adventure mad enough at the best of times, but in present conditions transcending all limits. For the sake of one intoxicating hour in this woman's arms, Loti risks not only his own head and several others, but every conceivable diplomatic complication. You will tell me that such conduct reveals appalling depths of selfishness. I do not deny it. But I have come to the conclusion that I have a right to do as I please, and that this insipid banquet of life requires all the spice that one can lend it.

You have nothing to complain of now, my dear fellow; I have written you a long enough letter. I do not count in the very least on your affection, or on anyone else's. But now and then, in this world, I have come across people whose talk and whose companionship have given me pleasure. You are one of them. Pardon this effusiveness. You can put it down to the Cypriot wine I have just been drinking.

The effect has worn off now. I went up on to the bridge for a breath of keen night air. Salonica was looking its shabbiest. Its minarets resembled a lot of old, half-burnt candles stuck in a dark and noisome town, infected with all the vices of Sodom. When the damp air strikes chill like an icy shower-bath and nature assumes her forlorn and dreary aspect, I shrink into my shell, where I discover only a sickening void and an infinite distaste for life.

I think of paying a visit to Jerusalem very shortly. There I shall try to recover some vestiges of faith. At present my religious and philosophical convictions, my principles of morality, my social theories, all have their apotheosis in one commanding personality, the policeman.

I shall probably be back in Yorkshire this autumn and shall look forward to seeing you.

Yours ever,

LOTI.

XI

Those last days of May 1876 constituted one of the stormiest phases of my existence. Such were my sufferings that they left me long afterwards crushed and listless, with a void at my heart. From this transitory lethargy I was presently roused by the vitality of youth. I awoke to find myself alone in life. My last hold on religion had vanished and with it every restraining influence.

On the ruins of my dead faith arose something akin to love. The Orient cast its glamour over this revival which took the form of a fever of the senses.

XII

With the three other wives in her master's harem, she had gone to live in a *yali* (country house) standing in a grove by the Monastir road. Here the supervision was less severe.

In the daytime I never went ashore unarmed. The cutter would land me right on the jetty among a crowd of boatmen and fisherfolk. Hovering about my path as if by accident, Samuel would watch for the signals by which I conveyed to him his orders for the night.

I have spent many a day wandering along the Monastir road. On either side lay a bare and desolate plain, with cemeteries, centuries old, stretching away into the distance beyond range of sight. Ruined marble tombs, their mysterious inscriptions eaten away by lichen; acres of granite menhirs, sepulchres—Greek, Byzantine, Mussulman—covered the ancient soil of Macedonia, where the great nations of the past have left their dust. Here and there rose the sharp silhouette of a cypress, or a great plane tree, with an Albanian shepherd and his goats resting in its shade. The parched earth was gay with great pale mauve flowers, diffusing a delicious scent of honeysuckle, drawn forth by a sun which was already scorchingly hot. The smallest features of that landscape are engraved upon my memory. With night, peace, balmy and inviolable, sank down upon the plain, a stillness broken only by the whirring of the cicala. The fragrance of summer hovered in the clear air; the sea was calm, and the sky as radiant as on tropic nights I have known of old.

She was not mine as yet. But all the barriers between us were down, save the material obstacles of her master's presence and the iron grating at her window. I spent my nights waiting for her, waiting for the moment, which was sometimes brief indeed, when I might touch her arm through those grim bars, and in the darkness kiss her white hands, bedecked with Eastern rings.

At a fixed hour before dawn, braving a thousand dangers, I would make my way back to the ship, with the friendly connivance of the officers of the watch.

XIII

I spent most of my evenings with Samuel. In his company I have witnessed many strange scenes in seamen's taverns, and have enjoyed almost unique opportunities of studying manners and customs in beggars' kitchens, and disreputable pothouses kept by Turkish Jews. On my visits to these dens I always wore the dress of a Turkish sailor, the least compromising guise in which to cross the Salonica roadstead by night. Samuel was a curious contrast to these surroundings. His pleasant, comely face seemed as if transfigured against that murky background. I was growing fond of him, and his refusal to have anything to do with my intrigue with Aziyadé increased my respect for him.

Ah, yes! we saw many a curious sight, my vagabond friend and I, in cellars, where strange orgies were held and men got dead drunk on mastic and raki.

XIV

One warm June night we two were lying out on the plain, waiting for two o'clock, the hour fixed for my return to the ship. I still remember that lovely starry night with never a sound save the low murmur of the slumbering sea. The cypresses flecked the mountain side with great black teardrops; the plane-trees were splashes of darkness. Here and there a pillar, centuries old, marked the forgotten haunt of some dervish of long ago. The dry grass, moss and lichen gave off a pleasant fragrance. On such a night it was bliss to be out in the open country. It was good to be alive.

This enforced vigil, however, seemed to have put Samuel in a villainous temper. He would not even reply when I spoke to him, so for the first time, I took a friendly grip of his hand, and said, in Spanish, words to this effect:

" My dear Samuel, you know you are used to sleeping either on the hard ground or on a plank. This turf is much more comfortable and has a delicious scent of thyme. Why don't you have a nap? You will wake up in a better temper. Are you vexed with me? What have I done to offend you? "

His hand trembled in mine and he returned its grasp with unnecessary violence.

" *Che volete?* " he asked in troubled tones, " *che volete mi?* What do you want with me? "

Some dark, unspeakable suspicion had flashed through poor Samuel's head. In those ancient countries of the East all things are possible. Then he buried his face in his arms, and lay there trembling, aghast at himself.

But ever since that strange moment, he has devoted body and soul to my service. Night after night, he risks life and liberty to enter Aziyadé's house. To bring her to me through the darkness, he runs the gauntlet of all the perils and ghostly visions that a certain cemetery holds for him. He rows about in his boat till dawn, keeping watch on our boat, or he waits for me on the fifth flagstone on the quay of Salonica, lying cheek by jowl with fifty vagabonds. He has, as it were, sunk his own personality in mine. Wherever I go, and in whatever disguise, there he is, shadowing me and ready to defend my life with his.

XV

Loti to Lieutenant Plunkett, R.N.

My dear Plunkett,

You can safely confide to me, without fear of boring me, all the ideas, fantastic, grave or gay, that flit through your head. I think of you as one apart from the vulgar herd and it will always be a pleasure to read anything you write to me.

Your letter was handed to me at the end of a dinner cheered with Spanish wine and I remember being at first a little taken aback by its singularity. You are certainly rather a character, but I was already aware of that. You are an intelligent fellow, too, as everyone knows. But there was something else I read between the lines. I realised that you must have gone through much suffering, and this fact is a link between us.

It is ten long years since, like yourself, I too was launched upon life in London and left to my own devices at sixteen. I have tasted a little of all the pleasures of life. On the other hand, I believe there is hardly a single pang that I have been spared. I feel appallingly old, though my fencing and acrobatics have kept me, physically, amazingly young.

Confidences, however, are superfluous. The mere fact that you have suffered is a bond of sympathy between us. I have been fortunate enough, I gather, to inspire you with some affection. I thank you. If you like, we will conclude an intellectual friendship, as you call it, and this pact of ours will help us through the dreary episode of life.

On the fourth page of your letter, your pen must have run away with you. You used the expression " Boundless affection and devotion." If you really meant it, you must admit that some of the bloom of youth is still upon you and that all is not yet lost. No one is more aware than I am of the charm of those wonderful, lifelong friendships. But you see, they happen at eighteen. At twenty-five you have done with that sort of thing. Thenceforth all one's devotion is required for self. It's a heartbreaking admission, but, alas ! only too true.

XVI

There was a great charm about those early morning expeditions which took me to Salonica before sunrise. The air was so sparkling, the coolness so delicious, that I could feel stealing over me a sense of wellbeing, which made me half in love with life. Turks in robes of red, green or orange were beginning to show themselves in the arcades of the bazaars, which lay shadowy and dim in the liquid half-light of dawn.

Thompson, the engineer officer, played the part of comic opera confidant to my rôle of *jeune premier*. Together we rambled through all the old streets of that city, and this at the most unlawful hours and in the most unorthodox attire.

The evenings held for us new enchantments. All was rose and gold. Mount Olympus, flushed with the red of burning embers or molten metal, was reflected in a sea as smooth as glass. There was not the slightest trace of haze in the air. It was as if atmosphere no longer existed ; the mountains stood forth in a perfect void, so clear and keen were even the remotest peaks. We spent

many an evening sitting among the crowds on the quay,
looking out over that peaceful bay. The barrel organs of
the East ground out their weird melodies, to a tinkling
accompaniment of Chinese bells. The cafés blocked the
public way with small ready-laid tables, which were all
too few to satisfy the demands for narghilehs, syrups,
lakoum and raki.

We made Samuel proud and happy by inviting him
to our table. He was always in the offing, waiting for a
chance to convey to me by signals the trysting place
Aziyadé had appointed.

Trembling with impatience I would dream of the
coming night.

XVII

Salonica, 1876.

Yesterday evening Aziyadé told Samuel to remain
with us. I looked on with surprise, as she asked me to
sit between herself and Samuel and began to converse
with him in Turkish. She wanted a talk with me, the
first we had ever had, and Samuel was to act as inter-
preter.

All that month, though united in the ecstasy of the
senses, we had been unable to interchange a single
thought, and until that evening had remained to each
other strangers and unknown.

" Where were you born? Where did you live? How
old are you? Have you got a mother? Do you believe
in God? Have you ever been in the black men's country?
Have you had many mistresses? Are you a lord in your
own land?"

She herself was a young Circassian, who had been
brought as a child to Constantinople with another little
girl of her own age. She had been sold to an old Turk,
who brought her up to give to his son. But the son died
and so did the old Turk. She was then sixteen and
extremely pretty. So her present master, who had seen

her at Stamboul, took possession of her and brought her back with him to his house at Salonica.

"She says," Samuel translated, "that her God is not the same as yours, and that she is not sure, from what the Koran says, whether women have souls like men. She is afraid that after you have gone away, she will never meet you again, not even when you are both dead, and that is why she is crying. Now," added Samuel, laughing, "she wants to know if you would mind jumping into the sea with her this very minute, so that you may sink to the bottom together, clasped in each other's arms. . . . Afterwards I am to take the boat back and say I never saw you."

"Certainly, I shall be delighted," I replied, "if only she will stop crying. Let us jump in now and get it over."

Aziyadé understood. Trembling she threw her arms round my neck and we both leaned out over the water.

"Don't do that," exclaimed Samuel in terror, holding us back in an iron grip. "It would be a horrible embrace. Drowning people bite each other and make ghastly grimaces."

He spoke in Sabir, with a barbaric crudeness impossible to reproduce in French.

.   .   .   .   .   .

It was time for Aziyadé to go. A moment later she had left us.

XVIII

London, June 1876.

My dear Loti,

I vaguely remember sending you a letter last month with neither head nor tail to it, neither rhyme nor reason —one of those letters written upon impulse, when the imagination gallops ahead and the pen toils behind, trotting or even limping, like a sorry old hack.

Such letters are never read over before they are sealed, or they would never be sent. Pedantic digressions with no particular point; absurdities that would have disgraced Tintamarre, and to crown it all I must needs pose as a much misunderstood person and blow my own trumpet with a view to evoking the sympathy and flattering remarks you were kind enough to tender. In a word, it was all supremely ridiculous.

Then those protestations of devotion! That was where old Rosinante took the bit between his teeth, for once. Your comments on this part of my letter are in the vein of that old writer, who lived sixteen hundred years before our era and tried his hand at everything,— at being a great king, a great philosopher, a great architect, at owning six hundred wives, and so on, till at last he grew so sick and weary of it all, that in his old age, after mature deliberation, he vowed that all was vanity.

There was nothing that I did not know before in that reply of yours, couched in the style of Ecclesiastes. I am so entirely of your way of thinking about everything and the rest, that I am afraid I shall never be able to argue with you, except after the fashion of the gendarme Pandore with his sergeant. We have absolutely nothing to learn from each other in the moral category.

" Confidences," you observe, " are superfluous."

To this also I bow. I like to take a general view of persons and things and to get an idea of the broad outlines. I have always had a horror of details.

" Boundless affection and devotion ! " Well, why not? It was one of those generous impulses, one of those luminous flashes, which reveal a nobler self. At the moment of writing one is sincere enough, believe me. If they are the merest gleams, who is to blame? You and I, who are in no way responsible for the deep imperfections of our nature? The Creator, Who designed us only to leave us rough-hewn and unfinished, capable of the noblest conceptions but without the power to fulfil them?

Or, rather, is there no one to blame? With so little to go upon, perhaps we had better leave it at that.

I am much obliged to you for your remarks on the ingenuousness of my emotions. I do not, however, plead guilty. They have seen too much service, I have made too many calls upon them, for them not to show signs of wear and tear. I might describe them as sentiments reserved for special occasions, and let me remind you, that there are moments, when a display of emotion is justified. You must admit, too, that there are things that gain in solidity in proportion as use rubs off their gloss and glitter. To take an illustration from the noble profession we both follow, you have only to think of seasoned cordage.

Well, then, it is agreed that I am very fond of you, and we need never refer to it again. Once and for all, let me assure you that you have great gifts and that it would be a thousand pities if you sacrified that which is best in you to your passion for acrobatics. Having thus unburdened myself, I will stop boring you with my protestations of affection and admiration, and tell you a little about myself.

Physically I am very fit, and am taking steps to secure health of mind. The cure consists of ceasing to rack my brains and of putting a curb on my emotions. In this world it is all a question of balance, both within and without. If one's sensibility gains the upper hand, it is always at the expense of one's reason. The better poet you are, the worse mathematician you will prove. A small amount of geometry is needed in life, and, alas! a large amount of arithmetic. I believe, heaven forgive me! that I have written you something approaching common sense.

Yours ever,

PLUNKETT.

XIX

Salonica.
July 27th. Night.

About nine o'clock all the officers go off to their quarters, after wishing me good-night and good luck. By this time, every one of them knows my secret.

I look anxiously at the sky above old Mount Olympus, whence all too often those great coppery clouds drift across, big with thunder and lightning and torrential rain. This evening, however, all is serene in that quarter. The crest of that mountain of myth and legend stands out in bold relief against the infinite blue of the sky.

I have been down to my cabin to dress and am on deck again. Now begins the anxious vigil of every evening. One hour, two hours, go by, and each lagging minute seems as long as a whole night. About eleven o'clock I catch the soft splash of oars falling on a slumbering sea. A tiny, faraway speck is coming nearer, stealing over the water like a shadow. It is Samuel with his boat. The sentries cover him with their rifles and challenge him. Samuel makes no reply; nonetheless the rifles are lowered. The men have private instructions, which apply only to Samuel. He is now alongside. Nets and other fishing tackle are handed to him, ostensibly for my use, and thus appearances are preserved. I jump into the boat and we push off. I throw off the cloak which covers my Turkish dress, and the transformation is now complete and my gold-embroidered tunic glitters faintly in the darkness. The breeze is warm and soft. Samuel pulls towards the shore without a sound.

A second little boat is waiting there, its occupants a hideous old negress with a blue cloth wrapped round her, an aged Albanian servitor picturesquely attired and armed to the teeth, and finally a feminine form, so closely veiled that she looks a mere shapeless bundle of white.

The negress and the Albanian are transferred to the other boat and without a word Samuel rows off with them. I remain alone with the veiled lady, who is as mute and motionless as a white phantom. I take the oars and we sheer off in the opposite direction, towards the open sea. With my eyes intent on that mysterious form, I eagerly await her first movement or gesture. When she thinks we have gone far enough, she holds out her arms to me. This is her invitation to come and sit beside her. I tremble as I touch her, and at once an overpowering languor begins to steal over me. Her veil is steeped in the perfumes of the East. How cool, how firm she is to touch!

I have loved another woman more, one whom I have forfeited the right ever to see again. But never before have my senses known such intoxication.

XX

Aziyadé's skiff is heaped with cushions, silken rugs, and Turkish coverlets. It is fitted with every luxurious device that appeals to Oriental languor and is more like a floating bed than a boat.

We are curiously situated. We dare not exchange one syllable of conversation. Every conceivable form of danger lurks around this couch of ours, which is drifting at its own sweet will over the depths of ocean. It is as if we had met together solely to taste the intoxicating delights of the impossible. In three hours comes the moment of parting, when the Great Bear has wheeled round in the depths of the sky. Each evening we watch its never varying course; it is the gnomon on the dial, by which we reckon our hours of bliss. Till then we are oblivious of the world, of life itself. Our lips meet in a kiss, which lasts from dark till dawn, seeking to slake a thirst akin to that burning thirst of African deserts, which draughts of cool water do but inflame and satiety itself can never quench.

At one in the morning the stillness of the night is broken by the startling sound of harps and women's voices, mingled with warning shouts which we have barely time to obey. A cutter from the *Maria Pia* passes us at top speed, with a select party of ladies and Italian officers, most of whom are drunk.   They just miss running us down.

XXI

We returned to Samuel's boat when the Great Bear had dipped to its lowest point on the horizon. The crowing of cocks could be heard in the distance.

Samuel lay wrapped in my cloak asleep in the stern-sheets. The old negress was asleep in the bow, huddled together like a monkey, while the Albanian sat in the middle nodding over his oars.

The two attendants rejoined their mistress and the boat bore Aziyadé silently away. For a long time I followed with my eyes that white form lying so still where I had left her, warm with my kisses, with the night dew upon her garments.

It was striking six bells on board the German warships. A pale light in the East threw into relief the sombre silhouettes of the mountains. Their base was hidden by the inky shadows they cast, which were reflected far down in the still depths of the water. In the gloom shed by these peaks it was impossible to judge distances.

The stars were fading. The damp chill of early morning descended upon the sea, and dewdrops clustered thickly on the planks of Samuel's boat. I was very lightly clad, with nothing on my shoulders but an Albanian shirt of thin muslin. I looked for my gold-embroidered tunic and found that I had left it in Aziyadé's boat. A feeling of mortal cold crept up my

arms and gradually pervaded my whole chest. I had still
an hour to wait for the moment when I could slip on
board without attracting the attention of the watch. I
tried rowing, but my arms were numb with an overpowering drowsiness. Then, very cautiously, I raised
the cloak under which Samuel was sleeping, and, without
disturbing him, crept in beside this friend of fortune's
providing. In less than a moment, in utter unconscious-
ness, we were both wrapped in that overwhelming sleep,
which there is no resisting. The boat drifted at random.

An hour later we were roused by a harsh Teutonic
voice hailing us. We had drifted into the midst of the
German ships. We seized the oars and hurriedly rowed
away, the watch covering us with their rifles. It was
four o'clock. Dawn was shedding its doubtful light on
the blur of white which was Salonica, and on the black
hulls of the battleships. I crept on board like a thief, only
too glad to have escaped notice.

XXII

The night afterwards, the night of July 28th, I dreamt
that I had suddenly to leave Salonica and Aziyadé.
Samuel and I were trying to run up the road to the
Turkish village where she lives, so that I might at least
bid her farewell. But we were both of us seized by the
paralysis that one experiences in dreams. The time was
slipping away and the corvette was shaking out its sails.

" I'll send you a lock of her hair," Samuel promised,
" a long brown tress."

And still we tried to run on.

Then I was awakened to go on watch. It was midnight. A seaman lighted my candle. It shone on the gilt
woodwork and the silken flowers of the tapestry, and I
was at once wide awake. It rained in torrents that night
and I was soaked to the skin.

XXIII

Salonica, July 29th.

At ten o'clock this morning I suddenly received orders to leave the corvette and Salonica and proceed by to-morrow's packet to Constantinople, there to join the *Deerhound*, the guardship patrolling the Bosphorus and the Danube. A party of seamen descended upon my cabin, tore down the hangings and packed the boxes. My quarters in the *Prince of Wales* were down below, a mere cubby-hole next to the powder magazine. I had furnished this den of mine, which never saw the sun, with a certain originality. The iron walls were hung with closely woven red silk tapestry patterned with fantastic flowers. Weapons, odds and ends of pottery, old knick-knacks newly gilded, shone out against this dark background.

In this dim room, I had gone through hours of suffering, those inevitable hours when a man communes with his own heart and is tortured with remorse and agonising regrets for the past.

XXIV

I had some good friends in the *Prince of Wales* and was in fact rather the spoilt child of the ship. But I have ceased to care for people and can part from them without regret. Here ends another chapter of my existence, and Salonica is yet another corner of the world that I shall never see again. Still, I have known ecstatic hours on the smooth waters of its great bay, nights for which many a man would have paid at a great price. I had almost come to love this girl, with her bewildering charm.

But before long I shall have forgotten those balmy nights, when the first ray of dawn found us lying in our boat, intoxicated with passion, while the morning dew lay thick upon us.

I shall miss Samuel, too, poor Samuel, who so freely risked his life on my account. He will cry like a child at my departure.

Here I am again, still letting myself drift, still letting myself be caught by every ardent affection or plausible imitation of it, however calculating and sinister its motive. Shutting my eyes, I clutch at whatever may fill, were it but for an hour, the terrible void of life. I embrace anything that masquerades as love or friendship.

XXV

Sunday, July 30th.

I left Salonica at noon on a day of blazing heat. At the last moment Samuel came alongside in his boat to take leave of me at the steamer. He seemed perfectly cheerful and unconcerned. Another who will soon forget me!

" Au revoir, *effendi, pensia poco de Samuel!* "

(" Farewell, my lord. Spare a thought sometimes for Samuel.")

XXVI

" In the autumn," Aziyadé assured me, " Abeddin Effendi, my master, is going to move his whole house-. hold, wives and all, to Stamboul. If by any chance he doesn't, I shall come by myself, for your sake."

Stamboul be it! I shall await her coming. But it means a fresh start, a new way of life, a new country, new faces, and Heaven alone knows for how long.

XXVII

The officers in the *Prince of Wales* gave me a great send off. Bathed in sunshine, the land gradually recedes into the distance. But for a long time yet I can make out the white tower where Aziyadé embarked at night, and the stony plain with its clumps of plane trees, which I have so often crossed in the darkness. Soon, all that remains of Salonica is a grey smudge, spreading over the sere and yellow mountains, a grey smudge bristling with black cypresses and white minarets. At last this, too, vanishes from my sight, doubtless forever, behind the highland of Cape Kara-Burnu. Above the coast of Macedonia, already far behind, tower the four great mountains of mythology: Olympus, Athos, Pelion and Ossa.

II

SOLITUDE

I

Constantinople, August 3rd, 1876.

The voyage took three days, with halts at Mount Athos, Dedeagatch and the Dardanelles. The passengers consisted of one fair Greek, two comely Jewesses, a German, an American missionary and his wife, and a dervish. A curious assortment, but we all got on very well and indulged in a great deal of music. General conversation was conducted either in Latin or in the Greek of Homer, while the missionary and I actually exchanged asides in Polynesian.

The last three days I have been staying, at Her Majesty's expense, at a hotel in Pera, where my neighbours at table are a noble lord and his amiable lady. She and I spend our evenings at the piano together, playing through the whole of Beethoven.

I am in no hurry for my ship to return from cruising about somewhere in the Sea of Marmora.

II

Samuel has followed me, like the faithful friend he is. I am touched by his devotion. He managed to creep on board another Messageries steam-packet and he presented himself to me this morning. I embraced him heartily. I was delighted to see his honest, open face again, the only friendly countenance in all this great city, where I do not know one living soul.

"There, Effendi," he said, "I have left everything, friends, country, boat, to follow you."

I have noticed that such instances of absolute and spontaneous devotion occur far more frequently among the poor than in other classes of society. I certainly prefer these humble people to respectable citizens, whose egotism and pettiness they do not share.

III

All Samuel's verbs end in *ate*. Everything that makes a noise is *fate boum*.

"If Samuel gets on a horse," he informs me, "Samuel always *fate boum*." (Tumbles off.)

His reflections are as spontaneous and inconsequent as a child's. He is frankly and ingenuously religious, full of the oddest superstitions, and practises all sorts of nonsensical observances. He is never more absurd than when he poses as a serious person.

IV

A letter from Loti's sister.

Brightbury,
August 1876.

My dearest brother,

Still at it! Darting and flitting this way and that, now settling for a moment, now off again, like a little bird that will not let itself be caught. Poor dear little bird, so wayward, so disillusioned, tossed by every wind, deceived by every mirage, and never able to find a resting place for weary head and quivering wing.

O those mirages, at Salonica or elsewhere!

On with the giddy whirl, till sick at last of your aimless
flight, you perch for good and all on some fair branch.
Your wings, I know, will never be broken, you will never
fall into the abyss; God, Who cares for little birds, has
spoken; His angels guard that dear but feckless head.

Farewell, my hopes! You will not come this year to
sit beneath the limes. Winter will be upon us without
your having set foot upon our lawn. For five years now
I have watched the flowers budding and the trees putting
forth their shade, with the delightful thought that I
should have *both* of you here. This hope was my happiness each summer season. Now only you remain, and we
are not to have the joy of seeing you.

I write to you from Brightbury, on a fine August
morning, sitting in our rustic drawing-room which opens
on to the courtyard with the lime-trees. The birds are
singing, and the sunbeams are dancing in every nook and
corner. It is Saturday, and from newly washed flagstones and boards rises a homely rustic appeal which I
know would touch your heart. The period of extreme
and suffocating heat is over, and we are entering upon
that season of peace and subtle charm, which may well
be compared to man's maturity. Flowers and greenery,
exhausted by voluptuous summer, now raise their heads
and break forth into new life. The colours are richer; the
verdure deeper; here and there an early yellow leaf em-
phasizes the virile beauty of nature's second blossoming.

All this little Paradise, dear brother, was waiting for
you; it seemed as if everything had bloomed for your
sake—and once again it will pass away without you. We
shall not see you. I must make up my mind to it.

V

The busy quarter of Taxim, on the high ground of
Pera. The carriages and dresses of Europe jostling the
costumes and vehicles of the East. Burning heat; a

blazing sun; a warm wind stirring up the dust and the yellow leaves of August; the scent of myrtle; the cries of the fruit sellers; the streets heaped with grapes and water-melons. These are the impressions my first glimpse of Constantinople has left upon my mind.

I whiled away several afternoons, sitting in the breeze beneath the shady boughs by the side of the Taxim road, an utter stranger to everyone I saw. As I pondered that last chapter of my life, I dreamily watched that cosmopolitan procession of passers-by. I was thinking chiefly of Aziyadé and was amazed to find her so firmly enthroned in the depths of my mind.

In this quarter of the town, I made the acquaintance of an Armenian priest, who taught me the rudiments of Turkish. I had as yet no particular liking for this country, which later I learnt to love. I viewed it as a mere tourist; and of Stamboul, where Christians feared to trust themselves, I knew practically nothing.

I spent three months in Pera, thinking out schemes for attaining that impossible dream of mine—I desired to make my home with her on the opposite side of the Golden Horn, to share her own Mussulman mode of life, to spend whole days in her company, to search the depths of her heart for those sweet, shy mysteries, of which I caught a glimpse in those nights at Salonica—to have her all to myself.

My house stood in a quiet corner of Pera, commanding a view of the Golden Horn and the distant panorama of the Turkish city. The splendour of summer lent a charm to this dwelling of mine. I worked away at Turkish, sitting at my great, open window, and I gazed down upon old Stamboul, which lay flooded with sunshine. Away to the northwest Eyoub stood out from the midst of its cypress groves. How sweet, I thought, to hide myself away with her yonder, in that mysterious, unfrequented spot, which would offer so strange and charming a setting to our love.

My house stood in the midst of great open spaces, full of tombs and cypresses, looking down on Stamboul. I have spent many a night roaming over these waste lands in the pursuit of some rash adventure with some fair Armenian or Greek. Deep in my heart, I remained true to Aziyadé. But day followed day and still she did not come. Of these damsels nothing remains, but that savourless memory, which is the aftermath of sensual passion. Apart from this, not one of them had the smallest attraction for me, and they were soon forgotten. Roaming about the cemeteries at night I had more than one awkward encounter. Once, about three in the morning, a man sprang out from behind a cypress and barred my way. He was a night watchman, equipped with a great iron-shod staff, a brace of pistols and a dagger, while I was quite unarmed. I guessed at once what he wanted with me. He would have attempted my life sooner than relinquish his prey.

I followed him docilely, for I had a plan of my own. We were walking on the brink of those precipices a hundred and fifty feet deep, which separate Pera from Kassim-Pasha. He was on the outside. I waited for a favourable opportunity and then flung myself at him. His foot slipped over the edge. He lost his balance and I heard him rolling right down to the stones at the bottom; there was an ominous thud, and then a groan. Comrades of his were doubtless close at hand. The noise of his fall would carry a long way through the silence of the night. I took to my heels and ran faster than any human foot could follow. In the east the night was already waning, when I reached my room. Unwholesome dissipation often kept me thus abroad in the streets till the small hours of the morning.

I had just dropped off to sleep, when I was roused by delightful music : human voices singing to the accompaniment of harp and guitar, a salute to the dawn, a lively Oriental melody, fresh as the morn itself. The minstrels

passed on and their voices died away in the distance.
Through the open window nothing was visible save
morning mist and the empty vaults of heaven. Then
suddenly, high above, like a rosy vision, minarets and
domes glowed forth. The whole Turkish town was
gradually outlined, hanging, as it were, 'twixt earth and
sky.

Then I remembered that I was at Stamboul and that
she had sworn to come to me.

VI

My encounter with the night watchman made a sinister
impression upon me. I gave up my midnight rambles,
and had no more mistresses, unless you count a Jewish
girl, called Rebecca, who lived in the Jewish quarter of
Pri-Pasha and knew me by the name of Marketo.

I spent the end of August and part of September
exploring the Bosphorus. The weather was warm and
radiant. The shady banks, the palaces and *yalis* were
mirrored in the calm blue waters, over which glided
gilded caïques.

Stamboul was busy with preparations for deposing the
Sultan Murad and consecrating Abdul Hamid.

VII

Constantinople, August 30th.

Midnight! The fifth hour by Turkish reckoning. The
night-watchmen strike the ground with their heavy iron-
shod staves. In the Galata quarter all the dogs are in
revolt and are uttering heartrending howls. Those in
my own district preserve a neutrality for which I am
grateful. Packs of them are sleeping outside my door.
Perfect calm prevails throughout the neighbourhood. I
watch the lights go out, one by one, in the three long
hours I spend lying by my open window.

The old Armenian houses at my feet are wrapt in
slumber and in darkness. I look out over a deep ravine,
at the bottom of which, like a splash of inky blackness,
lies a cypress wood centuries old. Ancient Mussulman
tombs rest beneath these gloomy trees, which at night
diffuse an aromatic perfume. From these heights I command the whole wide prospect, so pure and peaceful.
Beyond the cypresses, I can see the Golden Horn, a
gleaming sheet of water, and higher still on the skyline
looms the silhouette of an Oriental city, Stamboul itself.
The minarets, the lofty cupolas of the Mosques, stand
out against a star strewn sky, with a slender crescent
moon floating in its depths. The horizon is fretted with
turrets and minarets, faintly outlined in bluish tints
against the wan background of the night. The great
shadowy domes, that brood above the mosques, soar one
beyond the other as high as the moon itself, and impress
the imagination with a sense of gigantic size.

At this very moment a grim comedy is being enacted
down there in the Seraskerat, one of the imperial palaces.
The great Pashas have assembled in order to depose the
Sultan Murad. To-morrow Abdul Hamid will reign in
his stead. That Sultan, whose accession we hailed with
such enthusiasm three short months ago, who even to-day
was treated like a god, may be strangled this same night
in some corner of the Seraglio.

Yet all is still in Constantinople. At eleven o'clock
cavalry and artillery rattle past my house, at the gallop,
in the direction of Stamboul. Then the rumbling noise of
the batteries dies away in the distance and silence reigns
again.

Owls are hooting among the cypresses with the self-
same cry as the owls in the trees at home. I love this
summery sound, which wafts me back to Yorkshire, to
lovely evenings of my childhood under the limes in the
garden at Brightbury.

In the midst of this calm, images of the past rise vividly

before my eyes, the ghosts of all that is shattered, of all that is beyond recall.

I was expecting my poor Samuel back this evening; but I fear that I shall never see him again. My heart is heavy and my loneliness weighs upon my spirits. A week ago I let him sail with a ship bound for Salonica, so that he might earn a little money. The three boats, by which he could have returned, have arrived without him; the last one came in to-night and there was no one on board who had heard anything of him.

The crescent moon is slowly sinking behind Stamboul and the domes of the Suleimanieh.

I am a stranger and unknown in all this great city. My poor Samuel was the only one who knew my name or was aware of my existence. I was becoming genuinely fond of him.

Has he, too, deserted me, or has some accident befallen him?

VIII

It is the same with friends as with dogs. They always come to a bad end. It is better to have neither one nor the other.

IX

. . . . . .

The trusty Saketo, who comes and goes between Salonica and Constaninople on the Turkish steam-packets, is a frequent visitor of ours. Though shy at first, he soon began to feel at ease in my house. A good fellow, Saketo. He and Samuel have been friends since childhood, and he brings Samuel all the news from home.

Old Esther, one of those ancient Jewesses at Salonica, whose business it was to dress me as a Turk, sends me kind wishes and remembrances. She used to call me her *caro piccolo*.

Saketo is very welcome, especially when he brings me

the messages Aziyadé transmits to him through her negress.

" The *hanum* (Turkish lady)," he says, " sends greetings to Monsieur Loti and bids him not to grow weary of waiting for her. Before the winter comes she will be here."

X

Loti to William Brown.

I received your mournful letter only two days ago. You had addressed it to the *Prince of Wales,* and it went to Tunis and elsewhere.

You, too, poor fellow, have your burden of sorrow, and heavy enough it is. You feel it more keenly than others, because, unhappily for you, you like myself received the kind of education that makes for sensitiveness and a tender heart.

Doubtless you have kept your promises in all that concerns the woman you love. But what was the good? For whose benefit? On what moral grounds? If you care for her so deeply, if she loves you, too, do not let yourself be hampered by scruples or conventions. Take her, whatever the cost. You will be happy for a time; then you will be cured, and the consequences can take care of themselves.

I have been in Turkey ever since we parted five months ago.

At Salonica I met a young woman of extraordinary charm, Aziyadé by name, who helped to while away some months of exile; also a ragamuffin called Samuel, who has become my friend. I spend as little time as possible on the *Deerhound.* Like those intermittent fevers of Guinea, I put in an appearance every few days to do a turn of duty.

I have a shake-down in a part of Constantinople where

nobody knows me. Here I can follow my own bent, and I have at present a little Bulgarian girl of seventeen for temporary mistress.

The near East still keeps its charm; it has remained more essentially Oriental than one would have imagined. I have performed the unusual feat of learning Turkish in two months. I wear the fez and the kaftan and play at being an effendi, as children play at soldiers.

I used to laugh at those novels in which, after some catastrophe, pious people lose their delicacy of conscience and their moral sense, but perhaps my own case is not so very different from theirs. I no longer suffer; I no longer remember. I could pass by with indifference those whom I once adored.

I tried Christianity, but it was of no avail. That sublime illusion, which in some men and women—our mothers, for instance—fosters courage to the pitch of heroism, is denied me. Conventional Christians make me smile. If I were a Christian, nothing else would exist for me. I should at once become a missionary, and rush off somewhere or other to get myself killed for the cause of Christ.

Believe me, my dear fellow, time and dissipation are the two sovereign remedies. In the end, the heart grows callous, and then one ceases to suffer. This is no new truth; I am aware that Alfred de Musset would have put it better. But of all the old sayings, handed down from generation to generation, this is one of the eternal verities. That pure passion of which you dream is, like friendship, only a myth. Forget your idol for the sake of some light of love. If the ideal woman eludes you, take a fancy to the shapely limbs of some circus girl.

There is no God. There is no moral law. Nothing exists of all we were taught to reverence. We have but one short life, from which it is reasonable to extract all the pleasure we can, while we await the final horror of death.

The only real ills are sickness, ugliness, old age, and of these neither of us can complain. We can still have any number of mistresses; we can still enjoy life.

Let me open my heart to you and make my confession of faith. My rule of life is to do as I please, in defiance of all laws of morality and of all social conventions. I believe in nothing and nobody; I love nothing and nobody. I have lost both faith and hope.

It has taken me twenty-seven years to reach this stage. If I have sunk lower than most men, the heights on which I once dwelt were loftier than theirs.

My love to you.

LOTI.

XI

The mosque of Eyoub at the northwestern end of the Golden Horn, was built in the time of Mahomet II. over the tomb of Eyoub, companion of the Prophet. Access to it has always been forbidden to Christians, for whom even its immediate precincts are none too safe.

The mosque is built of white marble and stands in a lonely spot in the open country, with cemeteries surrounding it. Its dome and minarets are almost completely hidden in the dense verdure of a grove of huge plane trees and immemorial cypresses.

The cemetery paths, which are paved with stone or marble, lie deep in shadow and are for the most part sunk. On either side stand marble buildings of great age, their yet unsullied whiteness in striking contrast to the black tones of the cypresses. Hundreds of gilded tombs with borders of flowers encroach upon these gloomy paths; they are the sepulchres of the great, of the pashas of olden days and Mussulman dignitaries. The sheik-ul-islam have their funeral kiosques in one of these dreary avenues.

It is in this mosque of Eyoub that the sultans are consecrated.

XII

On September 6th, at six in the morning, I succeeded in penetrating into the second inner court of the mosque of Eyoub. The old building was hushed and empty. The two dervishes, my companions, were trembling all over at the audacity of our enterprise. Without a word we stepped across the marble flagstones. At that early hour, the mosque gleamed white as snow. Hundreds of ringdoves were fluttering about the deserted courts, picking up grain. The dervishes, in their rough serge robes, raised the leather curtain that hung over the doorway of the sanctuary, and permitted me to cast a glance into that holy of holies, the most sacred spot in all Stamboul, on which, until now, no Christian had ever set eyes. It was the eve of the consecration of Abdul Hamid.

I remember the day when the new Sultan went in great pomp to take possession of the imperial palace. I was one of the first to catch sight of him as he emerged from the old seraglio, the gloomy retreat where all the heirs to the Turkish throne are lodged. Immense caïques of state had come for him, and my own caïque actually grazed that of the prince.

These few days of power have already aged the Sultan. He has lost his former look of youth and spirit. The extreme simplicity of his dress contrasted with his new environment of Oriental luxury. This man, who was called from a state of comparative obscurity to the supreme power, seemed plunged in uneasy brooding. He was pale and thin, with a melancholy, abstracted air, and there were dark rings round his great black eyes. His face bore the stamp of breeding and intelligence.

The Sultan's caïques are manned by twenty-six oarsmen. They have the graceful lines that characterise all Oriental workmanship, and are magnificently decorated all over with gilding and carving; while the prows are of gold. The court lackeys wear a livery of green and orange, with quantities of gold and silver lace. The Sultan's throne is ornamented with several suns, and stands beneath a red and gold canopy.

XIII

To-day, September 7th, witnessed the great pageant of the Sultan's consecration.

Abdul Hamid, it seems, is all eagerness to invest himself with the prestige of the Khalifs. It may be that his accession will inaugurate a new era in the history of Mohammedanism, and lend to Turkey some lingering glamour, some last gleam of glory.

In the holy mosque of Eyoub, amid scenes of great pomp, Abdul Hamid girded on the scimitar of Osman. After this ceremony, he marched at the head of a long and brilliant procession all through Stamboul, on his way to the Palace of the Old Seraglio, pausing at every mosque and funerary kiosque in his path to pay the customary acts of worship and prayer. His bodyguard of halberdiers wore scarlet uniforms blazing with gold, and green plumes six feet high upon their heads. In their midst rode Abdul Hamid on a statuesque white steed with slow and stately paces, caparisoned with gold and gems. Behind him went the Sheik-ul-Islam in a green mantle, the emirs in cashmir turbans, the Ulema in white turbans with golden fillets, the great pashas and dignitaries, all of them on horses glittering with gold. A solemn and interminable procession, in which the most striking looking personages filed past. With servants to hold them on their quiet palfreys, octogenarian Ulema rode by, wagging their white beards and darting at the populace brooding glances fraught with fanaticism and mystery. The whole route was lined with dense masses of spectators, those Turkish crowds, whose brilliance puts to shame the most magnificent gatherings in Western Europe. The stands erected along a frontage of several kilometres were bending under the weight of eager throngs, arrayed in all the different costumes of Europe and Asia.

On the heights of Eyoub was massed a swaying multitude of Turkish ladies, their heads veiled with the white folds of the yashmak, while their graceful forms, in vivid silken draperies that swept the ground, could hardly be distinguished from the painted and chiselled tombstones beneath the cypresses. The effect was so dazzling, so fairylike, that it seemed not so much an actual scene as the fantastic hallucinations of an Oriental visionary.

XIV

Samuel's return has brought a little gaiety into my dreary house. I have had a run of luck at roulette, and autumn in the Near East is glorious. I am living in one of the loveliest countries in the world, and enjoying the most perfect liberty. I can explore at will villages, mountains, and forests on the shores of both Europe and Asia Minor. Many a poor fellow could feed his fancy for a year on the impressions I glean in the course of one day's rambles.

May Allah grant long life to Abdul Hamid, who has revived the great religious festivals and the magnificent ceremonies of Islam! Stamboul is illuminated night after night, and the Bosphorus is aglow with Bengal lights,—the last gleams of a vanishing Orientalism, a fairy spectacle, the like of which we shall doubtless never see again.

Although I care nothing for politics, my sympathies are with this splendid country, whose suppression has been agreed upon.

Gradually, almost unconsciously, I am becoming a Turk.

XV

Information on the subject of Samuel and his nationality. He is a Turk for convenience, a Jew by religion, and a Spaniard by virtue of his forefathers.

In Salonica he led a somewhat vagabond existence as a boatman and porter. Here, too, he picks up a living on the quays. He looks more respectable than his fellows, so he finds plenty of employment and does very well. In the evening he sups off a bunch of grapes and a hunk of bread, and then comes home to me, full of the joy of life.

My luck at roulette has deserted me, and we are both of us extremely poor. But our high spirits make up for it. Moreover, we are young, and pleasures, for which others have to pay dearly, fall in our laps.

When he goes to his work, Samuel puts on two pairs of ragged trousers, in the touching faith that the holes do not correspond, and that the demands of decency are satisfied.

Every evening, like two good Orientals, we may be seen smoking our narghilehs under the plane trees of a Turkish café, or visiting a puppet show to see Karagueuz, the Turkish Punch, who has a great fascination for us.

The general restlessness does not affect us, and as far as we are concerned politics do not exist.

The Christians in Constantinople are, however, in a state of panic. Stamboul inspires the residents of Pera with terror and they never cross its bridges except in fear and trembling.

XVI

Yesterday evening I rode through Stamboul to visit Izeddin Ali. It was the great festival of Bairam; the month of Ramazan was drawing to its close in a fairy-like scene of Oriental beauty. All the mosques were illuminated; the minarets glittering from base to topmost

turret; verses from the Koran in luminous letters fluttering in the breeze; thousands of men shouting with one
accord, at the firing of a cannon, the holy name of Allah;
crowds in holiday garb parading the streets with countless lights and lanterns, and veiled women moving in
companies to and fro, in silks that gleamed with silver
and gold.

Izeddin Ali and I wandered all over Stamboul and
finally, about three in the morning, wound up with a visit
to an underground den on the outskirts of the city, where
young boys of Asiatic race, dressed as nautch girls, performed unseemly dances to an audience composed of all
the sweepings of the Ottoman jails. To me it was an
orgy as disgusting as it was novel. I begged to be
excused the end of the entertainment, which must have
been worthy of the palmy days of Sodom. It was dawn
when we returned home.

XVII

KARAGUEUZ

The exploits and misdeeds of His Lordship Karagueuz
have entertained countless generations of Turks, and
there are no indications that his popularity is waning.
Karagueuz bears a strong family likeness to the French
Polichinelle and the English Punch. After beating
everyone, including his wife, he is himself beaten by
Shaitan—Satan—who in the end carries him off, to the
great delight of the spectators.

Karagueuz is made of cardboard or wood, and is produced either as a puppet play or a magic lantern show,
in both of which he is equally amusing. He hits upon
tones and postures of which our Punch has never
dreamed, and the caresses he lavishes upon his spouse are
irresistibly comical. Sometimes Karagueuz challenges

the audience and has a set to with the spectators. Now
and then he indulges in the most unseemly jokes, while
certain gestures of his would scandalise a Capuchin friar.
But it goes down very well in Turkey. No one objects.
Every evening the Turkish paterfamilias may be seen,
lantern in hand, taking a swarm of little children to see
Karagueuz. A hall full of babies looks on at a performance, which, at home, would make a corps of guardsmen
blush. This is a curious feature of Oriental morality,
from which it might be inferred that Mahommedans are
far more depraved than ourselves—an utterly erroneous
conclusion.

These theatres of Karagueuz open on the first day of
the lunar month of Ramazan and have a tremendous
vogue for thirty days. At the end of the month the
whole concern is taken to pieces and put away.
Karagueuz is shut up in his box for a whole year, and is
never, on any pretext whatever, allowed out again.

XVIII

I am tired of Pera and about to leave it. I am going
to take up my abode in old Stamboul, or rather on the
far side of Stamboul, in the sacred suburb of Eyoub
itself. There I am known as Arif-Effendi, and no one is
aware of my real name or social position. The pious
Moslems, my neighbours, are under no delusion as to
my nationality. But they care as little about it as I do
myself.

At Eyoub I am two hours away from the *Deerhound*.
I have a house all to myself, almost out in the open
country, in a Turkish quarter, which is picturesque to a
degree, with its rustic street humming all day long with
characteristic life; its bazaars, its cafedjis, its tents, its
solemn dervishes, smoking their narghilehs under the
almond trees. Its square, graced by an ancient, monu-

mental fountain of white marble, is the meeting place for all our visitors from the interior, gipsies, acrobats, bear-leaders. Here stands a solitary house, and this house is ours.

Downstairs there is the entrance hall, snowy with whitewash, and an empty room or two, which we never open, except in the evening before we go to bed, to satisfy ourselves that no one is hiding there. Samuel thinks that these rooms are haunted.

On the first floor there is my bedroom, with three windows opening on to the square, Samuel's little room, and the *haremlik* looking eastward over the Golden Horn.

The next flight of stairs leads to the roof, which has a terrace in Arab fashion, and is shaded by a vine. Most of the leaves, alas! have already turned yellow in the winds of November.

Close to my house stands the ancient village mosque. The muezzin is a friend of mine, and the top of his minaret is on a level with my terrace. When he has climbed its steps, before beginning his prayer, he always favours me with a friendly salaam.

There is a splendid view from my roof. Northwest of the Golden Horn stretches the gloomy plain of Eyoub, its sacred mosque rising in marble whiteness from the mysterious depths of a grove of immemorial trees; in the background lie desolate hills of sombre colouring, strewn with blocks of marble, the vast cemeteries that form a veritable city of the dead. Away to the east is the Golden Horn, with thousands of gilded caïques dancing on its waters; then the whole of Stamboul fore-shortened, mosques, domes and minarets, all huddled together in one confused blur.

In the far distance stands a hill covered with white houses. This is the Christian town of Pera, and some-where behind it is the *Deerhound*.

XIX

The sight of that empty house with its bare walls, its bleak windows, its doors without bolt or lock, overwhelmed me with depression. It was so far away, so very far way from the *Deerhound,* and the whole enterprise seemed so utterly preposterous. . . .

XX

Samuel has spent a whole week cleaning and whitewashing and stopping up chinks. We are having white mats nailed down over the whole floor, a Turkish practice, which is clean as well as comfortable. Window curtains and a wide divan covered in a material with a pattern of red flowers represent our first very modest attempt at furnishing.

The place looks different already. I see that I could make a home of this house, exposed though it is to all the winds of heaven. It seems to me less dreary than before. Nonetheless it cries out for the presence of one, who has sworn that she will come, and for whose sake alone, perhaps, I have cut myself off from the world.

At Eyoub I have become rather the spoilt child of the neighbourhood. Samuel, too, is very popular. Suspicious at first, my neighbours have now decided to overwhelm with kindness the charming stranger of Allah's sending whose domestic affairs puzzle them so hopelessly.

After a visit of two hours, the Dervish Hassan-Effendi delivered himself as follows:

" You are an incomprehensible fellow and everything you do is odd. You are very young, or at least you seem so. Yet you enjoy complete independence, such as even a man of mature years cannot always command. We have no idea where you come from, and you have no visible means of subsistence. You have already wandered over every quarter of the globe. You have amassed

more learning than even our Ulema. You know everything; you have seen everything. You are only twenty,
or, perhaps, twenty-two Yet a whole human life would
hardly suffice for all your mysterious past. Your place
is in the first rank of European society at Pera, and yet
you take up your abode at Eyoub, with the extraordinary
choice of a Jewish vagabond for companion. You are
an incomprehensible fellow. But I find pleasure in your
company and am delighted that you have come to settle
among us."

XXI

September 1876.

The ceremony of the Surre-humayun: the despatch
of the imperial gifts to Mecca.

Each year, a caravan loaded with offerings is sent by
the Sultan to the Holy City. Setting out from the palace
of Dolma-Bagche, the procession makes its way to the
quay of Top-Hane, where it embarks for Scutari in Asia
Minor. At the head goes a band of Arabs, dancing to
the throbbing of the tom-tom and flourishing long staves
with golden streamers. Camels with ostrich feathers on
their heads pace gravely along, carrying on their backs
erections of gold brocade and gems, which contain the
most valuable of the presents. The rest of the Khalif's
tribute is packed in chests of red velvet, embroidered with
gold, which are loaded on mules, bedecked with plumes.
The Ulema and great dignitaries follow on horseback,
and the whole route is lined with troops.

It is a forty days' march from Stamboul to the Holy
City.

XXII

On these November nights, Eyoub is a terribly dreary
spot. The first evening I spent in my hermitage, my
heart was heavy with strange forebodings. As soon as

I closed my door in the gathering darkness, a feeling of deepest melancholy wrapped itself around me like a shroud. I thought I would go for a stroll, and lighted my lantern—for anyone caught in the streets of Stamboul after dark without a light is clapped into prison. After seven in the evening, the whole of Eyoub is locked up and all is still. For the Turks bolt their doors and go to bed at sunset. Here and there you may see, in the light of a lamp, the shadow of a barred window upon the pavement. Do not look up. It is only a funeral lamp, and all that it illuminates is a row of huge catafalques, each surmounted by a turban. You might be murdered outside that barred window, to which you would look in vain for human aid. These lamps, twinkling there till dawn, are even more sinister than the darkness. At every street corner in Stamboul you will come across these mortuaries. Quite near us, where the streets come to an end, the great cemeteries begin. They are haunted by gangs of miscreants, who kill you, strip you, and bury you on the spot, without the Turkish police ever troubling their heads about it.

After asking me my business and receiving an answer, which seemed to him quite unintelligible and somewhat suspicious, a night watchman made me promise to return home. Luckily some of these men are very decent fellows, and this particular one, who was destined to witness many mysterious comings and goings, proved a model of discretion.

XXIII

" A companion you may find, but never a faithful friend.
    You may wander the whole world over and never make
        a friend."

                    —Extract from an old Oriental poem.

XXIV

Loti to his sister at Brightbury.

Eyoub, 1876.

. . . It becomes more and more difficult for me to open my heart to you, for every day your point of view and mine grow further apart. Long after I had ceased to believe, the idea of Christianity lingered in my mind with a vague and comforting charm. But to-day its presence has vanished utterly. I know nothing so idle, so false, so irrational. I have lived through some terrible moments, and have suffered cruelly, as you know.

I once told you that I should like to marry, and asked you to find me a bride, worthy of our ancestral home and our dear old mother. But now I would beg you not to trouble. I should make any woman I married unhappy. I would rather continue my life of self-indulgence. I write from my dreary house at Eyoub. Except for a small boy, Yusuf by name, whom I have taught to obey by signs, to save myself the trouble of talking, I spend long hours by myself without addressing one word to a living soul.

I told you I did not rely on anyone's affection. It is true. I have friends, who make a great show of devotion, but I do not trust it. Of them all, Samuel, who has just left me, is perhaps the one who cares most for me. But I am under no delusion. It is mere boyish enthusiasm on his part. One fine day it will all end in smoke and I shall be alone again.

In your affection, my dear sister, I do, to some extent, believe. It has the force of an old habit; and then one must needs believe in something. If you really care for me, tell me so, let me see it. I feel the want of someone to whom I may cling. If it is true, help me to believe it. The earth seems to be slipping from under my feet, the void is closing in upon me. I am in deep distress of mind.

As long as my dear old mother is alive I shall remain, to outward appearance, all that I am now. But when she has passed away, I shall come to bid you farewell and then I shall vanish and leave no trace behind. . . .

XXV

Loti to Plunkett.

Eyoub, November 15, 1876.

Behind all the Oriental phantasmagoria which surrounds me, behind Arif-Effendi, lurks a poor miserable devil with a mortal chill at his heart. There are not many people to whom this fellow, who is very reserved by nature, cares to unbosom himself, but you are one of them. Do as I may, Plunkett, I am not happy. I have discovered no expedient to distract my thoughts. My heart is full of bitterness and disgust.

In my loneliness I have come to depend on Samuel, that vagabond friend of mine, whom I picked up on the quay at Salonica. His heart is in the right place. As Raoul de Nangis might have said, he is a rough diamond set in iron. His society has a piquancy and freshness, which helps to banish my blue devils.

I am writing to you in the dismal hour of winter twilight. Everything is still, save for the voice of the muezzin, mournfully chanting in Allah's honour a plaintive hymn, centuries old. Images from the past come to haunt me with agonising vividness. Everything around me takes on a desolate and sinister look, and I wonder what on earth I am doing here, in this God-forsaken Eyoub.

If only she were here, my Aziyadé!

I am waiting and waiting—with the same success, alas! as Sister Anne.

I have just drawn the curtains and lighted the lamp and the fire. The setting has changed, and with it my mood. I continue my letter, seated by a cheerful blaze, with a fur coat round me and my feet on a thick Turkish rug. Just for fun I am pretending to be a dervish.

I hardly know what there is to tell you about my life that would amuse you. There is no lack of material; the difficulty is to choose. And then, the past is the past, you know, and ceases to be interesting.

Several mistresses, for none of whom I cared in the slightest; many rambles over hill and dale, expeditions on horseback and on foot; everywhere strange faces, indifferent or antipathetic; any number of debts; Jews on my tracks; gold-embroidered garments reaching to the instep, and in my heart and soul the emptiness of death.

Such is the situation this evening, at ten o'clock on November 15th. Squalls of wind and icy rain lash the windows of my desolate house. That is the only sound, and the old Turkish lamp hanging above my head is the only light at this hour in the whole of Eyoub. It is a gloomy spot, this Eyoub, the very heart of Islam, which contains the sacred mosque, where the Sultans are consecrated. Some fierce old dervishes and the guardians of the holy tombs are the only inhabitants of this quarter, which is the most fanatical and ultra Moslem district of the whole city.

As I told you, your friend Loti is all by himself, warmly wrapped in a coat of fox fur and ready to take himself for a dervish. He has bolted the doors and is revelling in the selfish luxury of his own fireside, which is all the more grateful, by contrast with the storm which is raging outside, in this perilous, inhospitable country.

Like all things of great age, this room of mine induces weird dreams and absorbing reveries. The carved oaken ceiling must have sheltered many strange inmates and witnessed many a drama. The local colour has been preserved. The floor is covered with mats and thick

Turkish rugs, the one luxury the house can boast, and, in Turkish fashion, we remove our shoes on entering, so as not to spoil the carpeting. Almost the only furniture is a very low divan, and there are cushions scattered about the room, which is steeped in the languid sensuousness of the East. Some weapons and a few old ornaments are hanging on the walls. Verses from the Koran, interspersed with flowers and grotesque beasts, are painted everywhere.

Adjoining my room is the *haremlik*, the women's quarters. Like myself, it is waiting for Aziyadé. If she had kept her promise she would be with me now.

The little room next to mine on the other side is likewise empty. It is Samuel's. Samuel has gone to Salonica to bring me news of my lady of the sea-green eyes. But it looks as if he, too, were not returning.

Supposing she never comes, why then, one of these days, someone will take her place. But it will be a very different thing. I have come almost to love this girl, and it is for her sake that I have turned Turk.

XXVI

To Loti from his sister.

———

Brightbury, 1876.

My dearest Brother,

Ever since your letter reached me yesterday I have been in the depths of despair! . . . Some day, perhaps not very far away, our dear mother will leave us, and then you will vanish out of my life forever. It would mean the blotting out of all our memories, of all our past. The old home at Brightbury would be sold and all our treasures dispersed. And yet you would still be alive, stagnating in some corner of the world, held fast in the clutches of Satan. I shall not even know your hiding-place. I shall only feel that you are growing old and that you are unhappy. Rather let God take you to Himself. In that case I should weep, but I should know that my loss was decreed. I should suffer, but I should acquiesce and bow my head.

I am horrified at what you have written. My heart bleeds for you. You could bring yourself to do this thing, since you say so. You could do it with unmoved countenace and stony heart. For you have made up your mind to follow a fatal and accursed path, and I no longer count for anything in your existence. . . .

And yet my whole life is wrapped up in yours. There is a secret corner of my heart where no one else may enter; it is your very own. When you desert me, you will leave it empty and it will ache and burn.

I am to lose my brother. You have warned me. It is only a matter of time, a few months perhaps. He is lost to me through time and eternity, and he has already died a thousand deaths. Everything is shattered; everything is in ruins.

Behold the beloved child sinking into the abyss, into the nethermost pit. He suffers; he has neither air, nor light, nor sun. But he is powerless. His eyes are fixed on the depths beneath his feet. He never lifts his head. He cannot. The Prince of Darkness has forbidden it. Now and then he still tries to resist. He hears a distant call; it is the voice that lulled him in infancy. But the Prince says to him: " Lies and delusions and vanity." And the poor child, bound and gagged in the bottom of the gulf, bleeding and forlorn, taught by his master to call good evil and evil good—what does he do? . . . He smiles.

Nothing surprises me from that tortured and labouring soul of yours, not even that cynical smile of Satan's teaching. How could you help it?

You have even lost, my dear brother, that yearning for a well-ordered life of which you spoke. You have no longer a desire for a dear little helpmeet, all modesty, gentleness, prettiness and charm, who would have borne you children for you to love. I used to picture her in the old drawing-room with the family portraits looking down on her.

The breath of corruption has passed over the scene. This brother of mine, whose heart cannot live without affection, this brother, with his hunger and thirst for love, now spurns such pure emotions. He will grow old with no one to cherish him, to smooth his brow. His mistresses will mock him. Who could expect them to do otherwise? And then, abandoned and despairing . . . then . . . he will die.

The more unhappy you are, the more troubled, bewildered and defiant, the more I love you. O darling brother, my beloved, if only you would come back to life! If only God would help you! If only you knew the desolation in my heart and the fervour of my prayers!

You shrink from conversion and all its tedium, from the grim aspects of Christian life. Conversion, that ignoble word! Tiresome sermons, stupid people, gloomy methodism, ascetism without colour and light, long words and all the evangelical cant! How could such things attract you?

But, you see, nothing of this is Christ; your idea of Him is utterly alien from that radiant Master Whom I know and worship. With Him you would experience neither fear, nor weariness, nor repulsion. In your mysterious sufferings, in your burning anguish, He would weep with you.

I am always praying for you, darling. Never have my thoughts been so full of you. It may be ten years, twenty years hence, but some day I know that faith will be given you. Perhaps I shall not live to see it. My life may not be long. But I shall never cease to hope and pray.

I have written a terribly long epistle. Such pages and

pages! What a bore to have to read them! I can see
my darling shrug his shoulders. Will there come a day
when he will no longer read my letters?

XXVII

"Old Kairullah," I said, "bring me women."

Old Kairullah was sitting on the ground at my feet,
curled up like some noxious and loathsome insect. His
bald, peaked head gleamed in the lamplight. It was eight
o'clock on a winter's evening, and Eyoub was as dark
and silent as the grave.

Old Kairullah had a son of twelve, called Joseph, an
angel of beauty, whom he was bringing up with the
tenderest care. Apart from this saving grace, he was the
vilest of mankind. He practised all the disreputable
trades of the outcast Jew in Stamboul and his own special
line brought him into touch with the Yuzbashi Suliman
and several of my Mussulman friends. None the less he
was generally tolerated and accepted, chiefly because, in
the course of time, people had grown used to the sight
of him. When you met him in the street you passed the
time of day with him, and even went so far as to touch
the tips of his hairy fingers.

Old Kairullah took some time to consider my request.

"Monsieur Marketo," he said at last, "women are
very expensive just now. But," he added, "there are
less costly diversions to be had; I could arrange for an
entertainment this very evening. . . . What do you say
to a little music?" . . .

With this cryptic utterance, he lighted his lantern, put
on his socks and fur-lined cloak and vanished.

Half an hour later the curtain over the door was raised
to admit six young Turkish boys in fur-trimmed dresses,
red, blue, orange and green. They were escorted by
Kairullah and another old man, even more repulsive than
himself. After much bowing the whole crowd sat down,

while I looked on, as impassive and motionless as an Egyptian idol.

All the children carried small gilt harps and they plucked at the strings with fingers laden with tawdry rings. A queer kind of music resulted, to which I listened in silence for some minutes.

" How do you like it, Monsieur Marketo? " old Kairullah whispered in my ear.

I had already grasped the situation, and I betrayed no surprise. Curiosity, however, impelled me to probe still further into this manifestation of human depravity.

" Old Kairullah," I said, " your son has more beauty than any of these."

Old Kairullah thought for a moment before replying.

" We can talk about that to-morrow, Monsieur Marketo." . . .

I drove out the whole pack like a herd of mangy cattle. Presently, however, I saw old Kairullah's head emerging, without a sound, from under the curtain over the doorway.

" Monsieur Marketo," he pleaded, " have pity on me. I live a long way from here and am supposed to have money. Better kill me with your own hand than turn me out at this hour of the night. Let me sleep in some corner of the house. I swear to be gone before daybreak."

I had not the heart to put the old ruffian out. He would certainly have died of cold and fright, even if he escaped being murdered. So I motioned him to a corner of the room, and there he crouched, all through that icy night, huddled together and rolled up like an old woodlouse in his shabby cloak. I could hear his teeth chattering and now and then a graveyard cough came from his chest. At last I took pity on him, got up again, and threw a rug over him.

As soon as the sky began to brighten, I bade him remove himself, with the advice never again to show his face inside my doors nor even to cross my path.

III

TWO IN EYOUB

I

Eyoub, December 4th, 1876.

She is here! For the last two days I have been living in a fever of expectation. This very evening a caïque is to bring her to the landing-stage at Eyoub, opposite my house.

My informant is Kadija, the old negress who, those nights in the boat at Salonica, used to bear Aziyadé company and risk her life for her mistress.

From three o'clock onwards I waited for her on the jetty. The day had been sunny and bright and there had been an unusual amount of traffic on the Golden Horn. Towards evening, thousands of caïques came alongside the Eyoub landing-stage, bringing the Turks from their business in the crowded centres of Constantinople, Galata and the great bazaar, back to their homes in the quiet suburb. I was beginning to be known at Eyoub, and some of the men hailed me.

" Good evening, Arif. What are you waiting for? "

They knew perfectly well that Arif could not possibly be my name, seeing that I was a Christian and came from Western Europe. But my Oriental pose no longer gave offence and they were pleased to call me by the name I had chosen.

II

> " Portia, heaven-lit torch! Portia,
> thy hand. 'Tis I."
>
> (*Portia, Alfred de Musset.*)

Two hours after sunset, one last, solitary caïque, coming from Azar-Kapu, drew towards the jetty. Samuel was at the oars. On the cushions in the stern reclined a veiled form. I saw that it was she! When the boat came alongside, the square surrounding the mosque was deserted and the night had turned cold. Without a word I seized her hand and ran with her to the house, giving no thought to poor Samuel, who was left outside.

When at last the impossible dream had come true, and she was there in the room I had prepared for her, alone with me, behind the ironbound doors, all I could do was to throw myself at her feet and clasp her knees. I realised how desperately I had longed for her. I was drowned in ecstasy.

And then I heard her voice. For the first time she spoke and I could understand—rapture hitherto unknown! But I myself could not utter one syllable of all the Turkish I had learnt for her sake; I could only stammer in English, as before, incoherent words I did not understand myself.

" *Severim seni,* Loti," she said. (Loti, I love you, I love you.)

Aziyadé was not the first to murmur these never-dying words to me. But never before had the exquisite music of love been wafted to my ears in the Turkish language. Delicious, half-forgotten music, can it be that I hear it again, gushing with such passion from the pure depths of a woman's heart, with such enchantment that I seem never before to have listened to it, that it thrills my disillusioned soul with the music of the spheres.

I lifted her in my arms, and held her so that the lamp-light fell upon her face and I could gaze at her.

" Speak again," I said, like Romeo. " Speak again."

I murmured in her ear many things that I felt she could not but understand. My powers of speech had returned and with them my Turkish, and I asked her question after question, imploring her to answer. But she only gazed at me in ecstasy. I saw that she had no idea of what I was saying, and that my voice fell upon deaf ears.

" Aziyadé," I cried, " don't you hear me? "

" No," she replied.

Then in her grave voice, she uttered these sweet, wild words : " *Senin laf yemek isterim!* " ("I wish I could devour the speech of your lips, Loti, and the sound of your voice.")

III

Eyoub, December 1876.

Aziyadé seldom speaks, and, though she often smiles, she never laughs. Her step is without sound; her movements are supple, sinuous, unhurried and inaudible.

This is a true picture of that mysterious little creature, who almost always slips away at dawn, to return at night-fall, the hour of phantoms and genii.

There is a dreamlike quality about her and she seems to cast a radiance whithersoever she goes. You look to see an aureole floating above that serious and childlike countenance. Nor do you look in vain, when the light catches those ethereal, rebellious, little curls, that cluster so deliciously about her cheeks and forehead. She thinks them unbecoming, and spends an hour every morning in unsuccessful efforts to plaster them down. This labour and the business of tinting her nails a brilliant orange are her two principal occupations. She is idle, like all women brought up in Turkey. But she can do embroidery, make rose-water and write her name. She scrawls it all over the walls, as solemnly as if it were a matter of vital importance, and she sharpens all my pencils for the task.

Aziyadé conveys her thoughts to me not so much with her lips as with her eyes. Their expression has extraordinary variety and eloquence. She is so expert in this language of the eyes, that she might use the spoken word less than she does or even dispense with it entirely. Sometimes she replies with a stave or two from a Turkish song. This trick of quotation, which would be tiresome in a European woman, has on Aziyadé's lips a curious Oriental charm. Her voice, though very young and fresh, is grave and its tones are always low pitched, while the Turkish aspirates lend it at times a certain huskiness.

This girl of eighteen or nineteen is capable of forming, on a sudden impulse, some desperate resolve, and of carrying it through in defiance of everything, even death itself.

IV

In the early days at Salonica, when I used to risk both Samuel's life and my own for the sake of one short hour with her, I had nursed this insane dream : to live with her in some remote corner of the East, where my poor Samuel could join us. This dream of mine, so contrary to all Mussulman ideas, so utterly impossible from every point of view, has come true in almost every detail.

Constantinople is the only place where such a scheme could have been attempted. It is a genuine wilderness of men, of which Paris was once the prototype, an aggregate of several large towns, where every man can lead his own life without interference, and assume as many different characters as he pleases—Loti, Arif and Marketo.

Blow, blow, thou winter wind! Let the squalls of December shake the bars on doors and windows.

Safe behind our massive iron bolts, with a whole

arsenal of loaded guns to protect us, and yet more secure
in the inviolable sanctuary of a Turkish dwelling—
warming ourselves at the copper brazier—is it not well
with us, my Aziyadé, in this home of ours?

V

Loti to his Sister in Brightbury.

My dear little Sister,

It was unkind and ungrateful of me not to write to
you sooner. You say I have made you very unhappy,
and I believe you. Unfortunately I meant everything I
said, and I still mean it. There is nothing I can do now
to relieve the pain I have given you. The mistake was
opening my heart to you in the first place, but you brought
it on yourself.

I believe that you care for me. Your letters alone
would convince me, if I had no other proof. I am very
fond of you, too, you know. You urge me to take up
some interest, some honourable and useful pursuit and
to throw myself into it, heart and soul. But I have my
dear old mother. She is now the one object in life to
which I devote myself. It is for her sake that I muster a
little cheerfulness and courage, and preserve the positive
and conventional side of my existence, as a lieutenant in
the Navy.

I agree with you. I can think of nothing more repulsive than a battered old roué, dying of dissipation and
exhaustion, and deserted by everyone. But that I shall
never be. When I begin to lose health, youth and love,
I shall disappear. You misunderstood me. By dis-
appearance I meant death. When I come home, I will
make one last effort for my mother's sake and yours.
Once more in the family circle, I may think differently.
If you will find me a girl, to whom you feel drawn, I

will do my best to love her, and, for your sake, to submit
to the bondage of affection.

I wrote to you about Aziyadé, so I may as well tell you
that she is here. She loves me with all her soul and never
dreams that I could ever bring myself to leave her.
Samuel, too, is back again, and, between the two, I am
surrounded with so much affection that I forget the
past—I forget ingratitude—I forget even my absent
friends now and then.

VI

From a modest beginning, Arif-Effendi's house has
gradually attained a certain luxury, with Persian rugs,
Smyrna curtains, weapons, and choice bits of pottery.
All these treasures have been acquired one by one, not
without some trouble, but this mode of collecting has
served to enhance their charm.

To roulette we owe the blue satin tapestry with the
embroidered red roses, once the pride of some seraglio.
The bare walls are now hung with silk. All this luxury,
hidden away in such a solitary, tumbledown house, pro-
duces the effect of some fantastic dream. Every evening
Aziyadé, too, brings some contribution. Abeddin
Effendi's mansion is, it seems, a perfect storehouse of
ancient treasures, and, according to Aziyadé, wives are
entitled to borrow from their masters' superfluity.

When the dream is over, she will restore all his
property, while everything of mine will be sold.

VII

What power on earth will give me back my life in the
East, my free life in the open air, and my desultory
rambles amid the stir and clamour of Stamboul? To set
out of a morning from Atmeidan with Eyoub for destina-
tion that evening; chaplet in hand to go the round of the
mosques; to look in at all the cafédjis; to linger by

sepulchres, mausoleums, baths, and squares; to sip
Turkish coffee from minute blue cups with copper
holders, to sit in the sun and smoke a narghileh till a
pleasing torpor ensues; to chat with dervishes and fellow-
wayfarers; to be free, light-hearted and unknown, and
to be oneself part and parcel of this kaleidoscopic scene,
so full of movement and sunshine! And all the time to
hug the thought that the beloved awaits one in one's own
house at nightfall. In Achmet I have a delightful companion on these wanderings. A true child of the people:
he is gay and dreamy by turns, poetic to a degree,
brimming over with laughter, and staunch till death.

The colours darken as we plunge deeper into the heart
of old Stamboul, and draw towards the sacred quarter
of Eyoub with its vast cemeteries. We catch an
occasional glimpse of the blue waters of Marmora and
the island and mountains of Asia Minor, but passers-by
are few and the sombre houses are stamped with the seal
of age and mystery. Everything we see could tell some
wild tale of ancient Turkey.

We dine where chance directs, sometimes at one of
the little Turkish booths, where Samuel has an eye to the
purity of the ingredients and himself superintends the
preparation of the meal.

It is usually nightfall when we reach Eyoub. We
light our lanterns as we turn towards the house, that
little home of ours so tranquil and secluded, of which
the very remoteness is one of its charms.

VIII

My friend Achmet is twenty, according to Ibrahim, his
old father; twenty-two according to his old mother
Fatma. No Turk ever knows his own age. Physically
he is a curious phenomenon, of small stature but of
Herculean strength. A stranger might conclude that he

had a delicate constitution, from the look of his thin, bronzed face with its tiny, aquiline nose, tiny mouth, and small eyes, now full of gentle melancholy, now sparkling with mirth and high spirits.

Take him all together, he has a curious charm. He is a strange lad, blithe as a bird, full of the queerest notions expressed in a new and original way, and he has quixotic ideas of honour and integrity. He has never learnt to read and spends his life on horseback. His heart is as open as his hand, and half his earnings go to the old beggar women in the streets. Two horses, which he hires out, constitute his entire property.

Achmet spent two days ferreting out my identity. He has promised to keep my secret, which is known only to him, on condition that in future he is admitted to terms of intimacy. He has gradually established himself as our friend, with his own place by our fireside.

He is Aziyadé's servant and knight. He adores her, and is far more jealous on her behalf than she is herself. In her interests, he spies upon all my movements, with the cunning of a practised detective.

" Let me be your servant instead of little Yusuf," he said one day. " He is dirty and dishonest. You can give me what you give him, if you insist on paying me. I shall be rather an odd sort of servant, but I shall live in your house and that will amuse me."

The following day I dismissed Yusuf, and Achmet took his place.

IX

A month later, with a deprecating air, I offered Achmet two medjidies for pay. Achmet, usually the soul of good temper, flew into a towering passion and broke two panes of glass, which he replaced the next day at his own expense. Thus the question of wages was settled,

X

I can still see him standing in the middle of my room
one evening and stamping his foot.

"*Sen chok shaitan, Loti! Anlamadun seni!*"

(" A perfect devil, that's what you are, Loti. You are
so deep, I can't make you out at all.")

His wide white sleeves flapped up and down with his
gesticulations of rage, and he shook his small head till
the silken tassel on his fez danced furiously.

He and Aziyadé had put their heads together to prevail
upon me to remain in Stamboul. He was to offer me half
his possessions, that is to say, one of his horses. I laugh-
ingly declined. Whereupon he declared that I was a
perfect devil and quite incomprehensible. Ever since
that evening I have been genuinely fond of him.

Dear little Aziyadé! She exhausted herself in tears
and arguments to induce me not to go. The dread of
my departure hung like a black cloud over her happiness.
At last, when she was quite worn out, she exclaimed :

"*Benim senim, Loti.* My soul is yours, Loti. You
are my God, my brother, my friend, my lover. When
you go, it will be the end of Aziyadé. She will close her
eyes and die. . . . But you must do as you please. You
know best."

" You know best "—an untranslatable phrase, which
means something like this :

" As for me, I am only a poor little girl who cannot
understand. I bow, with adoration, before your
decision."

" When you are gone," she resumed, " I shall wander
far into the mountains, and sing my song for you :

> " Shaitanlar, djinler,
> Kaplanlar, dushmanlar,
> Arslandar. . . .
> (Devils, genii, tigers, lions, human foes,
> Come not near my love.)

I shall die there in the mountains with that song upon my lips."

Then followed the song. She crooned it over every evening in a veiled voice. It was a long monotonous chant with a curious lilt to it and the disconcerting intervals and mournful cadences of Eastern music.

When I have left Stamboul and bidden her an eternal farewell, that song of Aziyadé's will haunt me for many a year in the watches of the night.

XI

To Loti from his Sister.

Brightbury, December 1876.

My dear Brother,

I have read and reread your letter. It is all I can ask for the present, and like the Shunamite woman gazing at her dead son, I can say:

" It is well with him."

Your poor heart is full of inconsistencies, like all distracted hearts, that drift without a compass. You utter despairing cries; you say that everything eludes you. You make an agonised appeal to my affection, and when I passionately assure you of it, you inform me that you are inclined to " forget absent friends," and that you are so blissfully happy in your corner of the East that you only wish the Paradise could last forever. Well, never mind. My affection will neither change nor waver. You will come back to it some day, when these idle pleasures are forgotten or have made way for others. Perhaps later on it will mean more to you than you think.

Dear Brother, you are mine; you are God's; you belong to both of us. I feel that some day, perhaps in the near future, you will recover courage, hope and faith. Then you will see how sweet and lovely, how healing and

precious that " delusion " may be. Thrice blessed falsehood, which gives me strength to live and die, without
fear, without regret; thrice blessed falsehood, which for
hundreds of years has governed the world, which has
inspired martyrs, created great nations, which changes
our mourning to gladness and proclaims throughout the
universe—Freedom, Love and Charity.

.   .   .   .

XII

To-day, December 10th, we paid a formal visit to the
Padishah.

Everything in the courts of the Dolma Bagche Palace
is white as snow, even to the pavement. Terraces, flagstones, steps, are all of marble. The Sultan's guards
wear scarlet, the musicians sky-blue laced with gold, the
footmen apple-green lined with capuchin yellow, and all
these gorgeous colours form a startling contrast to the
miraculous whiteness of the setting.

The angles of the pediments and the cornices of the
palace buildings serve as perches to family parties of sea-
gulls, storks and divers.

The interior of the palace presents a scene of extreme
splendour. Halberdiers, with towering plumes upon their
heads, are drawn up on either side of the staircases,
standing motionless like gilded mummies. Officers of
the guard, arrayed like Aladdin of the fairy tale, convey
their orders by gestures.

The Sultan looks pale and pensive; weary and
oppressed.

The ceremony is soon over. After a series of deep
bows, you back out of the presence, bending almost to
the ground.

Coffee is served in a great hall, overlooking the
Bosphorus. Kneeling servitors light for the guests
chibouks six feet long, with amber mouthpieces enriched

with jewels, and the bowls resting on silver trays. The *zarfs* (the coffee-cup holders) are of chased silver, set with large rose diamonds and many other gems.

XIII

You could search all Islam and never find a more unlucky husband than Abeddin-Effendi. He is always away in Asia Minor, poor old gentleman, and his four wives are none of them over thirty. By some miracle, they are all of them thick as thieves and are pledged to secrecy concerning one another's escapades.

Although she is by far the youngest and prettiest, even Aziyadé is not too unpopular, nor do her elders give her away. She is, be it noted, socially their equal. Thanks to some ceremony, of which the significance escapes me, she is entitled, like the others, to the appellation of lady and spouse.

XIV

" What do you do with yourself at home? " I asked Aziyadé. " How do you get through the long days in the harem? "

" It's very dull," she replied. " I just think of you, Loti, and look at your portrait, and play with the lock of your hair and all the little odds and ends of yours which I carry off to keep me company."

To own someone's portrait and a lock of his hair seemed to Aziyadé a very strange business indeed—something that she would never have dreamt of but for me, and contrary to all her Mussulman ideas. It was an innovation of the giaour, which had for her a fascination not unmingled with awe. She must indeed have loved me to let me cut off a long tress of her hair. She shuddered to think that she might suddenly die, before it had grown again, and she appear in the next world with a great lock shorn clean off by an infidel.

" But, Aziyadé," I pressed her, " before I came to Turkey, how did you pass the time? "

" In those days, Loti, I was hardly more than a child. The first time I saw you, I had spent but ten moons in Abeddin's harem and had not yet wearied of it. I stayed in my room, sitting on my divan, smoking cigarettes or hashish, or playing cards with Emineh, my maid, or listening to the queer stories about the black men's country that Kadija tells so well.

" Fenzile-hanum taught me to embroider, and we had visits to exchange with ladies in other harems. We had our duty to our master, and there was the carriage to take us for drives. Each wife is entitled to it in turn, but we all prefer to go out together and take our airings in company.

" On the whole we get on very well. Fenzile-hanum is very fond of me. She is the oldest and most important lady in the harem. Besmé is quick-tempered and sometimes flies into a rage. But it is easy to soothe her down and she soon gets over it. Ayesha is the most spiteful of the four, but she has to keep in with us and to hide her claws, because she is also far the naughtiest. Once she actually let her lover into her room."

It had long been a dream of mine, to slip, just once, into Aziyadé's room, to form an idea of the surroundings in which my darling spent her days. We had often discussed this scheme and Fenzile-hanum had actually been consulted. But we never carried it out. The more I know of Turkish customs, the more I realise how rash it would have been.

" Our harem," Aziyadé concluded, " is generally considered a model one, because we bear with one another, and keep on such good terms."

" A pretty sort of model! " I remarked. " Are there many like it in Stamboul? "

It was through the fair Ayesha-*hanum* that the contagion first crept in. In two years it has spread so rapidly, that the old gentleman's house is now a mere hotbed of intrigue, with all the servants corrupted. The great cage, despite its stout bars, is like a huge conjuring box, full of secret doors and back staircases. The captive birds can leave it with impunity, and fly off in every direction under the sun.

XV.

Stamboul, December 25, 1876.

Christmas Day! A fine night, clear, starry and cold. Leaving the *Deerhound,* I land at eleven o'clock at the foot of the old mosque of Funducli, with its crescent glittering in the moonlight.

Achmet is waiting for me, lantern in hand, and we wander up towards Pera, through the quaint old Turkish streets.

Great excitement among all the dogs! It is like roaming through the pages of a fantastic story, illustrated by Gustave Doré.

I am invited to a Christmas party in the European town, which will be the exact counterpart of every other Christmas party, held this evening in every nook and corner at home in England.

Ah! those Christmas Days of my childhood . . . those happy memories that still remain with me.

XVI

Eyoub, September 27, 1876.

Dear Plunkett,

Here's this unhappy Turkey promulgating a constitution. What is the world coming to? What is this century into which we have been born? A constitutional Sultan! Why, it upsets all my established notions.

Eyoub regards this event with consternation. All good Moslems believe that Allah has forsaken them and that the Padishah has taken leave of his senses. I, who see the humorous aspect of all serious matters, especially politics, feel that from the point of view of the picturesque, Turkey will lose much through the application of this new system.

I was sitting to-day with some dervishes in the funeral mosque of Suleiman the Magnificent. We mingled some politics with our discussion of the Koran, and agreed that neither that great monarch, who had his son Mustapha strangled before his eyes, nor Roxelane his spouse, who invented turned up noses, would have granted a constitution. Parliamentary Government will be the ruin of Turkey. There is no doubt about it.

XVII

Stamboul, September 27th.
7 Zi-il-iddjé 1293 of the Hegira.

I took refuge from a shower in a Turkish café near the mosque of Bayazid. Its only occupants were a few old greybeards in turbans (hajj baba), who sat reading the newspapers or looking out through the smoke-blackened windows at the passers-by, hurrying along through the rain. Turkish ladies, caught in the downpour, went tripping as fast as their babouches (heelless slippers) and pattens permitted. There was a great to-do and much hustling among the crowds in the street, while the rain continued to fall in torrents.

I scrutinized the old gentlemen around me. Their dress indicated a punctilious fidelity to the traditions of the good old days. Everything about them was *eski*, ◆ from their great silver-rimmed spectacles to the lines of their venerable profiles. *Eski*, a word uttered with reverence, means " antique," and is equally applicable in Turkey to old customs, old fashions in dress, and old materials. The Turks have a passion for the past, a passion for stability and stagnation.

Suddenly we heard the roar of a cannon, a salute of

guns from the Seraskerat. The old gentlemen exchanged significant nods and ironical smiles.

"All hail to the Constitution of Midhat Pasha!" exclaimed one of them with a sarcastic bow.

"Deputies! A charter!" muttered an ancient in a green turban. "The Khalifs of old had no need of representatives of the people."

"*Voï, voï, voï, Allah!* . . . Nor did our wives run about in gauze veils. The faithful said their prayers more regularly. And the Muscovites were less insolent."

The guns announced to the Moslems that the Padishah had granted them a constitution, which was on a more generous and liberal scale than any of the constitutions of Europe. But these old Turks gave a very cold reception to this boon of their sovereign's bestowing.

This event, which Ignatieff had done his utmost to postpone, had long been expected. It was equivalent to a tacit declaration of war between the Porte and the Tsar, and the Sultan was feverishly hurrying on his armaments.

It was half-past seven by Turkish time, that is to say, close on noon. The promulgation took place at Top-Kapou (the Sublime Porte) and thither I hurried through the deluge.

The Viziers, pashas and generals, the functionaries and authorities, all in full uniform glittering with gold lace, were assembled in the great square of Top-Kapou with the massed bands of the court in attendance. The sky was dark and stormy. Rain mingled with hail fell in torrents and drenched the whole audience. In this deluge, the reading of the Charter was vouchsafed to the people, while the old crenelated walls of the seraglio, which enclosed the scene, seemed to listen in amazement to these subversive utterances pronounced in the very heart of Stamboul.

Shouts and cheers and flourishes of trumpets brought this remarkable ceremony to a close. Then the crowds, soaked to the skin, tumultuously dispersed.

At the selfsame hour, in the Admiralty Palace at the other end of Constantinople, a meeting of the International Conference was in progress.

This combination of events was designed. The salvoes were to punctuate the address of Safvet Pasha to the plenipotentiaries, and to lend force to his peroration.

XVIII

"The East! The East! What see ye in the East?
Turn, poets, Eastward turn your eager gaze."
"Alas!" they cried, in voices long since mute,
"Though in the East mysterious day we see,
Perchance we take the twilight for the dawn."
(VICTOR HUGO. *Songs of Twilight.*)

I shall never forget the scene that evening in the great square of the Seraskerat, that immense esplanade on the central height of Stamboul, whence the sight travels across the gardens of the Seraglio to the faraway mountains of Asia Minor. The Arab porticos and the tall tower with its grotesque architecture were illuminated as on nights of high festival. The torrential rain during the day had turned the square literally into a lake, which reflected all these innumerable rows of lights. Against the far periphery of the skyline rose the domes of the mosques, the tapering minarets, each slender shaft decked with an ethereal coronet of fire.

A deathlike silence brooded over the square, which was utterly deserted. Right across the sky, swept clear by the winds of the upper air, ran two black bands of cloud, and above them the moon flaunted her bluish crescent.

It was one of those peculiar manifestations of nature, that are witnessed only in pregnant moments preceding some portentous event in the destiny of nations.

Of a sudden the stillness was broken by the tramp of footsteps and the sound of human voices. A band of softas (Moslem students of theology), carrying banners and lanterns, poured into the square through the central porticos.

"Long live the Sultan!" they shouted. "Long live Midhat Pasha! Hurrah for the Constitution! Hurrah for the War!"

These men were as if intoxicated with the idea that they were free at last. Only a few old Turks, mindful of the past, shrugged their shoulders as they watched these feverish crowds of enthusiasts.

"Let us go and salute Midhat Pasha," exclaimed the softas, and they moved off to the left through the mean little streets that led to the humble dwelling of the great Vizir, who was now at the height of his power, but only a few weeks later was to be driven forth into exile.

The softas, numbering about two thousand, proceeded to the great mosque, the Suleimanieh, to offer prayers. Thence they crossed the Golden Horn to Dolma Bagtche to acclaim Abdul Hamid. Outside the palace railings, deputations from every community joined forces with a huge and heterogeneous crowd in a spontaneous outburst of enthusiasm towards their constitutional monarch. Then they trooped back to Stamboul by the Great Pera road, stopping to bestow an ovation on Lord Salisbury, who was soon to become so unpopular, and on the British and French Embassies.

"Four hundred years ago," said the hojas haranguing the crowd, "our ancestors, a mere handful of men, conquered this land of ours. Shall we, who number some hundreds of thousands, suffer it to be invaded by the foreigner? Moslems and Christians alike, let us die for our Ottoman fatherland, rather than accept humiliating terms!"

XIX

The mosque of Sultan Mehmed-Fateh (Mehmed the Great) has often beheld Achmet and myself, basking in the sun outside its great portico of grey stone,—the two of us lying there without a care in the world, lost in some vague dream not to be expressed in human speech. The square of Mehmed-Fateh, which lies high above old Stamboul, consists of wide open spaces, which are frequented by men in cashmere caftans and great white turbans. In its centre stands one of the largest and most deeply revered mosques in all Constantinople. The immense square is girt by mysterious walls, which are topped by a line of stone domes, like a row of beehives. These are the softas' dwellings, which no infidel may enter.

This quarter is a centre of purely Eastern activity. Camels traverse it with leisurely gait, their bells tinkling monotonously. Dervishes sit there, deep in pious meditation, and as yet no tinge of Western Europe has entered it.

XX

Near this spot is a gloomy unfrequented street, all green with moss and grass. It is there that Aziyadé lives, and this is the secret attraction of the place. Here, where no one knows me and I am safe from all suspicion, I spend those long daylight hours when I may not be with her, and I feel that at least I am near her.

XXI

Aziyadé grows more silent every day and her eyes have a deeper sadness.

" What is the matter, Loti? " she asked me once. " Why are you always so sorrowful? It is I who should be unhappy, because I shall die when you go away."

She fixed her eyes on mine with a gaze so intent, and searching, that I turned away my head.

" I sorrowful, my darling? " I protested. " When you are with me, I ask nothing more. I am as happy as a king."

" True, Loti, for is any man better loved than you?
You need envy no one, not even the Sultan himself."

There she is right. The Sultan, the man whom
Ottomans account happiest of all created beings, does
not arouse my envy. The monarch has grown old and
tired, and a constitutionalist into the bargain.

" Aziyadé," I rejoined, " I think the Padishah would
give all his possessions, even his great emerald, which is
as big as my hand, his charter and his parliament, in
exchange for my youth and liberty."

" In exchange for you too," I nearly added. But
doubtless the Padishah would set but little store by any
woman, however charming, and I had a mortal horror
of uttering nonsense in the comic opera strain, for which
my costume was only too well suited. A looking-glass
showed me my own reflection, distressingly suggestive of
a young tenor about to warble a ditty by Auber.

There are times when I can no longer take my Turkish
rôle seriously. The ear of Loti sticks out beneath the
turban of Arif. I become sickeningly self-conscious and
am seized with a morose revulsion of feeling.

XXII

In the fashionable world of frock-coats and top hats,
I was always a man of arrogant and fastidious tastes.
No one was ever brilliant or distinguished enough for
my liking. I had the utmost contempt for my equals and
chose my friends from the fine flower of society. But
here I have become one of the people, a plain citizen of
Eyoub. I have adopted the homely way of life of the
boatmen and fisherfolk, and I take a true delight in their
society and their simple pleasures. Of an evening, in
the Turkish café kept by Suleiman, the circle by the
fire widens when I come in with Achmet and Samuel.
After shaking hands all round, I sit down to listen to
some tale from the Winter Nights, those long stories

about spirits and genii which take a whole week to tell. The hours slip by and leave no trace of weariness or regret. I feel perfectly at home in these surroundings, which have lost all trace of strangeness.

Although Arif and Loti are two entirely different persons, on the day that the *Deerhound* sails, Arif has only to remain in his house, where no one would dream of looking for him, and Loti vanishes, forever.

This idea, which originated with Aziyadé, sometimes presents itself to me with singular seductiveness. To stay with her, and to lead, not in Stamboul, but in some Turkish village by the sea, the healthy existence of humble folk, in the sunshine and the open air; to live from day to day, with no creditors to plague one, and no cares for the future! I am more fitted for such a life than for my present career. I have a loathing for all work that does not tax body and muscles; I detest all scientific pursuits, and all the conventional duties and social obligations imposed by Western civilisation. To be a boatman in a gold-embroidered tunic, somewhere in southern Turkey, where the sky is always clear and the sun always hot! After all, it could be done, and I should be less unhappy there than elsewhere.

" I swear to you, Aziyadé, that I would give up everything without a pang of regret—my social position, my name and country. As for friends, I have none; I can snap my fingers at them. But, you see, I still have my old mother."

Aziyadé no longer pleads with me to stay, though perhaps she has an inkling that the thing might not be utterly impossible. But she realises instinctively all that an old mother must stand for, this poor little orphan girl, who has never known one. These notions of generosity and self-sacrifice are more admirable in Aziyadé than in others, because they are spontaneous. No one ever took the trouble to inculcate these virtues in her.

XXIII

Plunkett to Loti.

——————

Liverpool, 1876.

My dear Loti,

Figaro was a man of genius. He laughed so much that he never had time to cry. His way is best; I realise this so thoroughly that I try to follow it myself, and not without success. Unhappily, however, I find it difficult to remain the same person for very long on end. Only too often, Figaro's high spirits desert me, and then it is Jeremiah, the gloomy prophet, who enters into me, or David, that august figure of despair, with the hand of the Lord heavy upon him. I cannot speak; I can only shout and rave. Nor can I write; I should only break my pen and hurl down the inkbottle. I stride up and down my room, shaking my fist at some unseen enemy, or at some imaginary scapegoat, whom I charge with all my sorrows. I commit the most desperate extravagances. Behind my locked door, I do the wildest things, till at last, calmed down, in other words, exhausted, I have relieved my feelings and am once more myself. Again you will call me a queer sort of crank, or a fool, perhaps. So I am, but not as big a one as you think—not nearly as big a one as you yourself, for instance.

Before passing judgment on me, you would have to know something about me and understand me a little; you would have to consider the circumstances that changed a reasonable human being into the eccentric creature he is now. We are, you see, the product of two factors, namely our hereditary tendencies, the endowment with which we enter upon the stage of life, and the circumstances that mould and shape us like some plastic substance, which receives and retains the imprint of everything that touches it. My own experiences have never been any-thing but painful. To use a hackneyed expression, I have been taught in the school of adversity. Whatever I have learnt, has been at my own expense, and I have mastered the lesson thoroughly. That is why I sometimes express myself rather forcibly. If now and then, I seem a trifle dogmatic, it is because I claim, by virtue of much suffering, to know more about things than do persons who have not gone through so much, and to be better qualified to speak than those who have not the same first-hand experience. For me this world holds out no hope; nor have I the consolations of those whom an ardent faith inspires with strength for the struggles of life and with trust in the supreme justice of the Creator.

And yet I can go on living without blaspheming.

But is it possible for any man, amid eternal tribulations, to preserve the illusions, the enthusiasms, the bloom of youth? As you are aware, I have renounced the pleasures proper to my years; they no longer appeal to me. I have lost both the looks and ways of a young man, and henceforth I must live on without purpose, as well as without hope. But does that mean that I am reduced to the same plight as yourself, sick of everything, denying all that is good, repudiating virtue and friendship and all by which we rise superior to the brute creation?

Let us understand each other, my friend. On those subjects I disagree with you entirely. In spite of all my experience of life (and may you never acquire the same knowledge! The process is too painful), I still believe in these things and in much else besides.

When I was in London, George showed me a letter from you. It begins very prettily with an account of an amourette in the Turkish style, elaborated and embellished with descriptions. We followed you, George and I, through the bewildering mazes of a huge Oriental anthill. We gazed with open mouths at the pictures you drew for us. Those three daggers of yours reminded me of the shield of Achilles, sung in such elaborate detail by Homer. And then, perhaps because you got a speck of dust in your eye, or because your lamp began to smoke as you were finishing your letter, or perhaps for some cause more trifling still, you must needs throw at our heads a whole set of eighteenth century platitudes. I really believe that the truisms of those ignoramuses, the Holy Fathers, are more profitable than those futile doctrines of materialism, which would result in the annihilation of everything that exists. The eighteenth century, however, accepted those materialistic notions. God was merely a superstition. Morality was only another name for expediency, and society had become one vast field of action lying at the mercy of any man with brains enough to exploit it. This group of theories appealed to many, because of its novelty and the sanction it accorded to the most immoral actions. A detestable epoch, in which there was no restraining influence and all things were permissible! A man could laugh at every-thing; nothing was too sacred—till at last so many heads had fallen under the guillotine of the revolution, that the few that survived began once more to reflect.

Then followed a period of transition. A generation arose, smitten with moral phthisis, afflicted with constitu-tional sentimentality. It lamented a past, of which it knew nothing; disparaged a present, which it did not under-stand, and distrusted a future which it could not divine. A generation of romanticists, of homuncules, who spent their days laughing and crying, praying and blaspheming, repeating their futile jeremiads in every key, till one fine day they ended by blowing their brains out.

Nowadays, my dear fellow, people are more rational and practical. Before you can attain your full develop-ment, you begin turning yourself as fast as you can into a selected type of humanity, or a highly specialised animal, if you prefer it. On every subject you acquire the opinions or prejudices suitable to your class. You drop into your proper sphere and adopt its traditions. Thus you develop a special habit of mind, or if you like, restrict your intelligence to suit your environment. Your fellowmen understand you; you understand them. You enter into intimate communion with them and become a true member of the fraternity. You may be a banker, an engineer, an official, a grocer, a soldier—anything you please. At all events you do something; you are somebody; your place is here and not elsewhere, and you do not lose yourself in dreams that lead nowhere. You have no misgivings. Your line of conduct is clearly indicated by the duties you are called upon to perform. Any doubts you may have, in the matter of philosophy, religion or politics, are smothered by the puerile amenities of society. Why bother your head about trifles? Civilisation has sucked you in. You are snatched up into the thousand and one wheels of the huge social machine, and are whirled through space, till at last your sensibilities are blunted, and old age comes to the rescue. You beget children, to grow up as dull as yourself.

In the end you die fortified with the rites of Holy Church. Your coffin swims in holy water. Latin chants are droned around your catafalque, where you lie in a blaze of candlelight. Those who were accustomed to seeing you about, will regret you, if you were a decent fellow when you were alive; some, it may be, will even mourn you sincerely. Finally your heirs succeed to your possessions. Such is life!

All this in no way belies the fact that there are some very excellent people here on earth, people who are thoroughly sound and honest, who do good for their own private satisfaction, who neither steal nor take life, even when they could do so with impunity, because they have a conscience which is a perpetual check on the promptings of their passions; people capable of affection, of wholehearted sacrifice; priests, who believe in God and practise Christian charity; doctors, who face epidemics to save a few humble patients; sisters of mercy, who venture amid the clash of armies, to minister to the wounded; bankers, to whom you may safely entrust your fortune; friends, who are ready to give you half of theirs; people,—myself for instance, to go no further afield—who, in spite of all your blaspheming, are capable of offering you boundless affection and devotion.

Put aside these caprices of yours, these whims of an ailing child. They all come from your habit of dreaming instead of thinking, of obeying your instincts, instead of listening to the dictates of reason. You libel yourself when you write such things. If I told you that I agreed to all you said at the end of your letter and endorsed your description of yourself, you would at once write to protest, and to assure me that you did not mean one word of your atrocious confession of faith. You would own that it was mere bravado on the part of one, who had a tenderer heart than most men; that it was only the painful effort of a sensitive plant, contracted with anguish, and struggling to recover itself.

No, my dear fellow, I decline to believe you. You do not believe yourself. You are good and affectionate and responsive. Only, you are unhappy. And so I forgive you, and remain devoted to you, a living refutation of your denial of everything in the way of friendship and disinterested affection. It is only your vanity that speaks, not your real nature. Your wounded pride bids you hide the treasures of your heart, and flaunt a fictitious self, the morbid creation of arrogance and boredom.

Ever yours,

PLUNKETT.

XXIV

Loti to William Brown.

My dear Brown,   Eyoub, December 1876.

This is to remind you that I am still in the land of the living. I am known by the name of Arif Effendi,

and have a home in the Kuru Chechmeh street at Eyoub.
I should much appreciate a sign of life from you.

Landing on the Stamboul side of Constantinople, you
pick your way through three miles or so of bazaars and
mosques, till you reach the sacred suburb of Eyoub,
where the children make your outlandish headgear a
target for their pebbles. You enquire for the Kuru
Chechmeh street, which is at once pointed out to you.
At the far end of this street, you will come upon a marble
fountain in the shade of almond trees, and just beside it
is my house.

This is where I live with Aziyadé, the girl from
Salonica, of whom I used to tell you, and whom I have
come perilously near to loving. I am almost happy in
this spot, which induces oblivion of the past, with its
burden of ingratitude.

I need not bore you with the details of my removal to
this faraway corner of the East, and of my decision to
adopt for awhile the language and customs of Turkey,
and even its delightful silk and gold attire.

I will begin with this evening, December 30th. The
weather is cold and clear and there is bright moonlight.
Off the stage may be heard the monotonous chant of the
dervishes, a familiar sound which rings daily in my ears.
My cat Kedi Bey and my servant Achmet, one in the arms
of the other, have just gone off to their joint bedroom.

Reclining like a true daughter of the East on a heap
of rugs and cushions, Aziyadé is busy tinting her nails
a bright orange, an operation of the highest importance.

And I, I sit here thinking of you and of those days in
London, and of all our escapades. I write in the hope
of getting an answer out of you.

I have not yet turned Mussulman for good, though
you might have supposed so from the beginning of this
letter. I merely impersonate two different characters,
and am still officially, though as seldom as possible, Loti,
the naval lieutenant.

As it would puzzle you to reproduce my address in Turkish, you may direct your letter to me under my real name, either to the *Deerhound* or to the British Embassy.

XXV

Stamboul, January 1st, 1877.

The year 1877 opened with a glorious, springlike day. After paying some visits in Pera, prompted by a lingering regard for the customs of Western Europe, I rode home to Eyoub in the evening, by way of the cemeteries and Kassim-Pasha.

I passed the terrible Ignatieff in his brougham. He was returning hot haste from the Conference, attended by a strong escort of Croats, all of whom were in his pay. A moment later I caught a glimpse of Lord Salisbury and the British Ambassador, likewise homeward bound, and both in a great state of perturbation. There have been heated discussions at the Conference, and things are going as badly as possible.

The unfortunate Turks reject with the energy of despair the conditions imposed upon them, and in return for their trouble, they are to be declared outside the pale of the law.

Should this come to pass, all the Ambassadors, with a warning shout of " Every man for himself " to the European colony, would with one accord take their departure. Terrible scenes would follow : a general upheaval attended with frightful bloodshed. May we be spared such a calamity ! It would mean my leaving Eyoub—perhaps within twenty-four hours—with no hope of ever returning.

XXVI

One glorious evening we were wandering down the slopes of Oun-Capan.

From the top of every minaret the *hojas* were intoning

unfamiliar prayers to strange chants; their strident voices, launched from those airy heights at such an unusual hour of the night, produced a disturbing impression upon the mind. The Moslems were standing in knots outside their doors, and all of them seemed to be watching some alarming portent up in the sky.

Achmet followed their glances and then clutched my hand in terror. The moon, which a moment ago we had seen shining so radiantly on the dome of St. Sophia, was now blotted out, yonder in space. All that remained of her was a lurid, reddish blot, the colour of blood.

There is nothing so startling as such signs in the heavens, and my own first impression, which flashed like lightning through my head, was likewise one of dismay. It was so long since I had looked at an almanack, that I was quite unprepared for the phenomenon.

Achmet explained to me what a grave and ominous matter it was. According to Turkish superstition, the moon is at grips with a dragon, which is seeking to devour her. A rescue, however, may be effected, by calling upon Allah and by firing at the monster. Special prayers were even now being offered in every mosque and a fusillade had begun all over Stamboul. From every window and roof, guns were being fired at the moon, in the hope of bringing this dread portent to a happy issue.

At Phanar we hired a caïque to take us home, but were presently ordered to halt. Half way across the Golden Horn, we were held up by the Zaptiyehs' boat. During an eclipse it is forbidden to be out in a caïque. At the same time, we could hardly be expected to sleep in the street. We argued the case and took a strong line with these gentry, and once more put up a successful bluff.

On reaching the house, we found Aziyadé waiting for us in fear and trembling. All the dogs were lugubriously baying at the moon, and this added to the general confusion.

Achmet and Aziyadé, with an air of mystery, informed

me that the dogs were howling in order to obtain from Allah a miraculous bread, invisible to human eyes, which is granted to them only on certain solemn occasions.

In spite of the fusillade the eclipse has become complete. The whole disc is now suffused with a peculiarly intense shade of red, which is due to special atmospheric conditions. I attempt to explain the phenomenon in the usual schoolroom fashion by means of a candle, an orange and a looking-glass. I exhaust all my arguments but fail to convince my pupils. They cannot accept my preposterous hypothesis that the earth is round. With an air of dignity, Aziyadé goes back to her cushions and flatly declines to take me seriously. I feel detestably like a schoolmaster. In the end I burst out laughing, eat the orange, and give up my demonstration.

After all what is the good of all this stupid science? Why should I try to cure these two of superstitions, which to my mind only enhance their charms?

So here we are, all three of us, firing out of the window at the moon, which still looms blood-red in the midst of glittering stars, in the most radiant of skies.

XXVII

Towards eleven o'clock, Achmet wakes us up to tell us that the treatment has been successful and the moon has recovered. Sure enough, there she is, her old self again, blazing like some wonderful, bluish lamp, in the glorious Eastern firmament.

XXVIII

" My Mother Behijé " is a very remarkable old lady, despite her infirmities and her eighty years. Daughter to one pasha, wife to another, she is more Mussulman than the Koran itself, and more bigoted than even the Law of the Beloved.

Shefket-Daoub Pasha, her late husband, was a favourite of Sultan Mahmud and had a hand in the massacre of the Janissaries. Behijé Hanum, who was at that time in her husband's confidence, urged him to this step with all her powers of persuasion.

This ancient lady lives in a precipitous street in the Turkish quarter of Janghir on the heights of Taxim. Her house is built on the very brink of an abyss, and for even greater security, its two projecting *shaknisirs* are strongly fortified with bars of ashwood.

This eyrie commands a view sheer down upon Funducli, the Dolma Bagche and Cheraghan palaces, Seraglio Point and the Bosphorus, with the *Deerhound* lying there, like a black nutshell on a blue cloth—and thence to Scutari and the whole coastline of Asia Minor.

Behijé Hanum spends her days in this observation post, reclining in an armchair. At her feet, a frequent visitor, sits Aziyadé, watching for the smallest sign on the part of her revered friend, and drinking in her words as if they were the inspired utterances of an oracle.

It is a curious phenomenon, the friendship between these two, this humble little girl and the Cadi's widow, that stern and haughty dame of noble race and lofty house. Behijé Hanum is known to me by hearsay only. No infidel is ever admitted to her house. In spite of her four-score years, she still has beauty, so Aziyadé assures me : " the beauty of a glorious winter night." Whenever Aziyadé comes out with some new idea, or some deep or illuminating comment, on matters of which she cannot possess the slightest knowledge, I ask :

" Where did you get that, my darling? "

And the answer is always the same.

" From my Mother Behijé."

" My Father," " My Mother " are titles of respect applied in Turkey to all aged persons, whether you know them or not.

Behijé Hanum is decidedly no mother to Aziyadé;

or at best, she is a remarkably imprudent one, who never scruples to rouse her child's youthful imagination to a pitch of feverish excitement. On the subject of religion, she works upon Aziyadé's feelings, till the poor, forlorn girl sheds bitter tears over her love for an unbeliever. She turns Aziyadé's little head with long romantic stories, told with much spirit and wit, of the great Chengiz and the desert heroes of old, and Persian and Tartar fairy tales about young princesses who are persecuted by genii, but perform, nonetheless, prodigies of fidelity and courage. All these legends are repeated to me, of an evening, by the dewy lips of my love.

Whenever Aziyadé comes home to me in a state of unusual excitement, I can always safely say:

" To-day, my little friend, you have spent your time sitting at the feet of Mother Behijé."

XXIX

January, 1877.

All the week I have been away at Buyukdéré on the upper Bosphorus at the mouth of the Black Sea. The *Deerhound* is anchored close to the great Turkish iron-clads, which are stationed there, like watchdogs, to keep an eye on Russia. This move on the part of the *Deerhound*, which took me away from Stamboul, coincided with a visit of old Abeddin to his house. So all is for the best. The enforced separation obviated the need for prudence on our part.

It is rainy and cold. I spend my days roaming the forest of Belgrade, and my woodland rambles bring back to me the happy days of my childhood. The old oak trees, the holly, the moss and ferns are almost identical with the flora of Yorkshire. Were it not for the bears that haunt it, a man might fancy himself back in the dear old woods at home.

XXX

Samuel is afraid of kédis (cats). In the daytime, kédis put funny ideas into his head, and he cannot help laughing when he looks at them. At night, however, he keeps at a respectful distance. One evening I was dressing for a ball at the Embassy, when Samuel, who had just left me to go to bed, suddenly came back and knocked at my door.

" *Bir Madame Kédi,*" he said in consternation. " *Bir Madame Kédi qui portate ses piccolos dormir com Samuel.*"

(" Here's a lady cat, who has brought her kittens to sleep in Samuel's bed.")

" In my family," he continued with a perfectly solemn face, " anyone who disturbs a cat, dies within a month. What am I to do, Monsieur Loti? "

When I had finished dressing, I decided to lend my friend a helping hand and went into his room. Sure enough there was a cat, who had taken up her position right in the middle of his pillow. She was of matronly plumpness, with a beautiful yellow coat, and was sitting up with a triumphant and dignified air, keeping her eye now on the petrified Samuel, now on the kittens, which were playing about all over the counterpane.

Samuel had retired to a corner and was sitting there, dropping with sleep, looking on at this scene of domestic bliss with mingled resignation and dismay. He was waiting for me to come to the rescue.

I had not the pleasure of Madame Kédi's acquaintance. She made no protest, however, when I lifted her onto my shoulder and put her and her kittens outside. After carefully shaking the counterpane, Samuel made as if to go to bed.

I had not intended to return to the house that night, but I changed my mind and came back again about two in the morning. Samuel had thrown his window wide open, put up clothes-lines, and hung out all his bedding, to let the fresh air cleanse it from any remaining taint of cat. He had then taken possession of my bed, and was sleeping the sleep of youth and innocence. Which was all very well for him. . . .

The next day we discovered that Madame Kédi, despite her roving habits, was the cherished pet of an old Jew of the neighbourhood, who made a living by renovating tarbooshes.

XXXI

It was the Greek Christmas, and high festival was being held throughout old Phanar. Troops of children, carrying lamps and paper windmills of every shape and colour, paraded the streets and hammered at every door with might and main, delivering earpiercing serenades to the thumping of a drum. The Byzantine doors, crumbling away with age, were thrown open; girls in Paris frocks appeared in the massive embrasures and threw copper piastres to the musicians. Yet, in spite of all this boisterous merrymaking, old Phanar could not contrive to throw off its sinister aspect. Achmet, who was with me, displayed the utmost contempt for the rejoicings of these infidels. Things were far worse, however, when we reached Galata. No other spot on earth can raise a more diabolical uproar nor exhibit such a spectacle of squalid misery. There was a seething mob, composed of every nationality under the sun, but with the Greek element greatly predominating. From all the slums, pothouses and taverns issued in solid masses a filthy rabble of Greeks. No imagination could conceive such a welter of intoxicated men and women, or such drunken and disgusting yelling and screaming.

There were a few good Moslems about, who had come to enjoy a quiet laugh at the expense of the infidels and to see how the Levantine Christians, whose fate, described in such pathetic orations, had moved all Europe to tears, celebrate the nativity of their Prophet.

These men, who were panic-stricken at the prospect of being forced to fight like the Turks, have been indulging in a perfect orgy of rowdyism and drunkenness, ever since the Constitution has bestowed upon them the title of citizen, which they have done nothing to deserve.

XXXII

I remember that evening when the baykush (owl) followed our caïque over the Golden Horn. It was a cold night in January. An icy mist merged all the massive outlines of Stamboul into one confused blur, and descended on our heads in a fine drizzle. Achmet and I rowed in the direction of Eyoub, taking turns at the oars. It was pitch dark, when we drew alongside the Phanar landing-stage, carefully groping our way among piles and wreckage and thousands of caïques that lay stranded on the mud. The spot was just at the foot of the old walls of the Byzantine quarter, where, at so late an hour, there is never a human soul to be seen. But for all that, two women were waiting there that evening, two shadowy forms with white-veiled heads, crouching in a certain dark corner beneath the balcony of a ruined house. They were Aziyadé and her faithful old Kadija.

Aziyadé entered the boat and we pushed off again. It was a long way still from the Phanar landing-stage to Eyoub. Here and there a lamp, burning in the house of some Greek, cast upon the turbid waters a streak of yellow light. Except for these occasional gleams, all was black as midnight.

As we passed an old house braced with iron, we heard a band playing dance music. Someone was giving a ball in one of those great mansions, so forbidding without, so luxurious within, where the old Greek families of Phanar hide their wealth, their diamonds, and their Paris gowns.

The festal sounds died away in the mist and once more we were swallowed up in darkness and silence. A bird came and circled heavily round our boat, passing hither and thither above our heads.

" *Bou fena!* (a bad business)," exclaimed Achmet, shaking his head.

" Baykush mi? (Don't say it's an owl)," said Aziyadé, from the depths of her multitudinous wraps.

When it was a question of their own beliefs and superstitions, these two always discussed them with each other and ignored me altogether.

Presently she took my hand.

" *Bou chok fena, Loti. Ammâ sen . . . bilmezsen!* "

(" It's very bad, Loti . . . but of course you don't understand these things.")

For all that, it gave one an eerie feeling to have this bird hovering around on a winter's night. It followed us without a moment's respite for the space of an hour or more, the time it took us to row from Phanar to Eyoub. There was a tremendous current running that evening in the Golden Horn. The icy drizzle continued. Our lantern was out, which made us liable to arrest by the bashibazouks of the patrol, and this would have spelt ruin for all three of us.

Near the Balat ferry we met caïques full of Jews, who at this point occupy both banks, Balat and Pri-Pasha. You meet them of an evening, returning home from the great synagogue or from visits to one another. This is the only part of the Golden Horn where one encounters any traffic at night. They passed us singing a plaintive song in their own language. The baykush was still hovering above our heads, and Aziyade was weeping with cold and fright.

What a relief it was, when in utter silence and pitch darkness, we made our caïque fast at the Eyoub jetty! To cross the mud, jumping from plank to plank—each one of which we knew blindfold—to traverse the deserted square; softly unfasten locks and bolts and secure them again behind us; cast a glance into the shadowy rooms on the ground floor, the space under the stairs, the kitchen and the inside of the oven; discard our muddy boots and wet garments; walk barefoot up the carpeted steps; bid good-night to Achmet, who goes off to bed; enter our own room, again turning the key; let down the white and red Arab door curtain, and subside on to the pile of thick rugs in front of the copper brazier, which had been alight ever since morning, diffusing a grateful warmth, impregnated with the scent of rose water and seraglio pastilles—all this meant to us, for twenty-four hours at least, safety and the infinite bliss of being together.

But the baykush had followed us and now began to hoot in the plane-tree under our windows. With that boding cry in her ears, Aziyadé, utterly worn out, cried herself to sleep.

XXXIII

" Our Madame " (bizum Madame), as Samuel and Achmet called her, was an old hag, who had traipsed all over Europe and tried her hand at every trade. An Italian by birth, she could speak every language under the sun and she kept a disreputable café in the Galata quarter. The café faced a wide and busy thoroughfare; it was very roomy and ran a long way back. At the far end another door opened on to a blind alley of evil reputation, adjoining the Galata quay. This alley served as outlet to several houses of ill-fame, while the café was the favourite haunt of certain Italian and Maltese merchant seamen, who were suspected of smuggling and thieving. Business of various kinds was transacted within its doors and everyone venturing there at night did well to carry a revolver.

Our Madame was very fond of all three of us, Samuel, Achmet and myself. It was generally she who prepared the meals for my two friends, whose business often kept them late in this quarter of the town.   She lavished maternal attentions on all three of us.

On the first floor there was a small closet, containing a trunk.   This was my changing room.   I would come in at the front door in European dress, and go forth the complete Turk by the blind alley at the back.

XXXIV

Yesterday that monstrous farce, the International Conference, ended in smoke.   The thing having missed fire completely, their Excellencies are off; the Ambassadors are packing up and the Turks are now outside the pale of the law.

A pleasant journey to all concerned !   Happily we are to remain.   At Eyoub everyone is perfectly calm and collected.   Every Turkish café, however mean, serves in the evening as a common meeting place for all sorts and conditions of men, rich and poor, pashas and humble citizens alike : there is an equality, such as our own democratic nation and the republics of Western Europe have never known.

Among them there is always some scholar to interpret the cryptic utterances of the daily papers.   Everyone listens with silent conviction.   There are none of those heated arguments, inspired by ale or absinthe, which are the rule in every bar at home.   Eyoub takes its politics seriously.   Why despair of a people which remains loyal to so many of its principles, and shows such earnestness and singleness of purpose ?

XXXV

To-day, January 22nd, the ministers and great dignitaries of the Turkish Empire met in solemn conclave at the Sublime Porte, and unanimously voted the rejection of the proposals made by the European Powers, beneath which they seemed to see the claws of Holy Russia. These men, who have come to this desperate resolution, are inundated with congratulatory addresses from every corner of the Empire. Patriotic enthusiasm ran high in this assembly, which witnessed for the first time in history an amazing scene : Christians and Moslems sitting side by side; Armenian prelates fraternising with dervishes and the *Sheik-ul-islam,* while Mussulman lips uttered the incredible words : " Our Christian brethren."

A tremendous impulse towards fraternity and union was welding together all the different religious communities of the Ottoman Empire, in the face of a common peril. The Armenian Bishop addressed to the assembly the following remarkable and martial harangue :—

" Effendis ! For five centuries the ashes of our forefathers have reposed within the earth of our native land. Our first duty is to defend this soil which is our heritage. Death is inevitable. It is the law of nature. History has shown us how great nations have arisen, one after the other, and in due course vanished from the face of the world. If Providence in its wisdom has ordained the downfall of our country, we can but bow to its decree. But there is a difference between ignoble extinction and a glorious end. If the fatal bullet awaits us, let us, as in honour bound, meet it breast forward, not turn our backs to it. Then at least our name will figure heroically in the annals of history.

" But a little while ago we were a lifeless body. The charter, which has been granted unto us, has reanimated and consolidated this body. To-day, for the first time, we have been summoned to this council, by the grace of His Majesty the Sultan and the Ministers of the Sublime Porte. Henceforth let all religious questions be relegated to the domain of conscience. Let the Mahommedan betake him to his mosque, the Christian to his church.

But for the sake of the common cause, in the face of our
country's foes, let us be united and so remain."

XXXVI

Aziyadé had remained faithful to the little yellow
morocco babouches, the heel-less slippers which are part
of the dress of all good Mahommedan ladies. She wore
out quite three pairs a week. There were always spare
ones lying about in every corner of the house, with her
name written inside, in case Achmet or I should be
tempted to steal them.

A terrible doom awaited all the discarded slippers.
They were hurled by night from the top of the terrace
into space and ended in the Golden Horn. This proceeding was called the *kourban,* the immolation of the
babouches. On very cold, clear nights, it was fun to
climb the old wooden stairs that creaked beneath our feet,
up to the roof, and there in the radiant moonlight, after
satisfying ourselves that all the neighbourhood was wrapt
in slumber, to execute the *kourban* and send each poor
little slipper spinning into the air. Where would it come
down: in the water, on the mud, or on the head of a
prowling cat? In the intense stillness, the sound of its
fall told us which of us two had guessed right and won
the bet.

It was delicious up there, on the housetop, all alone,
my love and I; so peaceful, so remote from the rest of
humanity. Now and then a carpet of spotless snow was
spread beneath our feet, and we gazed down upon old
Stamboul deep in repose.

It was not given to us to rejoice together in the sun-
light. Other lovers could wander arm in arm in the
glory of the day, without ever realising their good
fortune. But the terrace on the roof was our only
promenade. Up there we could breath the keen, pure
air of glorious winter nights, with the moon, discreetest

of duennas, for a third, now sinking slowly westwards
towards the lands of the unbelievers, now rising, a disc
of red, in the eastern sky and illuminating the far away
silhouettes of Scutari and Pera.

XXXVII

" Is this the end, O Lord, or the beginning? "
—VICTOR HUGO. Songs of Twilight.

There is great activity on the Bosphorus. All day
long, transports, packed with troops for the front, are
arriving and departing. They come pouring in, soldiers
and reservists, from every part of the Empire, the interior of Asia Minor, the borders of Persia, and even
Arabia and Egypt. They are hurriedly equipped and
dispatched to the Danube or to camps in Georgia. Each
batch of troops is speeded on its way with loud flourishes
of trumpets and awe-inspiring shouts to the honour of
Allah. Never has Turkey seen so many of its sons
under arms, all of them so full of courage and resolution.
Allah alone knows what will become of all these
multitudes.

XXXVIII

I should never have forgiven their Excellencies, had
their diplomatic pasquinades interfered with my private
life. I am glad enough to find myself back in my little
secluded house, which, it seemed at one time, I might
have to leave. It is midnight. As I write, the bluish
rays of the moon are stealing across my paper; the cocks
have begun their nightly concert. Here at Eyoub, a man
is very far from his own kind, and, at night, he is very
much alone; but the peace he enjoys is compensation.
Sometimes I can hardly believe that Arif Effendi is really
Loti, and I have grown so sick of the latter individual,

after twenty-seven years of his company, that I am content now and then to imagine myself someone quite different. Aziyadé is away in Asia Minor. The whole harem is on a visit to another harem at Ismidt. I expect her back in five days' time. On the floor beside me lies Samuel, sleeping as calmly as a child. To-day he saw a drowned man fished out of the water, and the sight was so horrible that he was frightened. He therefore thought it advisable to bring his mattress and blankets into my room.

To-morrow, at peep of dawn, the reservists bound for the front will resume their shouting, and all the mosques will be crowded. Gladly would I go with them and like them lay down my life, on some front or other, in the Sultan's service. It is a splendid and stirring spectacle, this struggle of a people that refuses to accept its doom. Turkey inspires in me something of the enthusiasm I should feel for my own country, were it confronted with a similar menace and in like peril of death.

XXXIX

Achmet and I were lounging in the square of the mosque of Sultan Selim. We were following with our eyes the twists and turns of the old stone arabesques, climbing up the grey minarets, and the curls of smoke, rising from our chibouks into the limpid air. All round the quadrangle runs an old wall, which is pierced here and there by doors with pointed arches. Not many pass this way. A tomb or two lies in the shade of the cypress trees. It is Turkey, pure and simple. One might easily fancy oneself two centuries back.

" Well, Loti," said Achmet truculently, " I know what I shall do when you go away. I shall have a glorious spree, and get drunk every day. I shall hire an organ-grinder to follow me round and play from morning to night. I shall spend all my money, but I don't care (*zarar yok*). I am like Aziyadé. Your departure will be the end of your friend Achmet, too."

I had to make him promise to be sensible, but it was no easy task.

"Will you give me a promise in return, Loti?" he said. "When you are married and rich, will you come back and fetch me, and let me be your servant over there? You shall not pay me wages, any more than you do in Stamboul, but I shall be near you and that is all I ask."

I promised to give Achmet a home beneath my roof and to entrust my children to his care.

The prospect of bringing up my offspring and adorning them with the fez, was sufficient to restore his spirits. We spent the whole evening evolving schemes of education, which had at least the merit of originality.

XL

Plunkett to Loti.

My dear Loti,

If I did not write to you, it was merely because I had nothing to say. And when this is the case, I usually hold my tongue. After all, what was there to tell you? That I had many things to occupy me, none of them pleasant? That I was " in the fell clutch of circumstance," whence escape is difficult? That I was languishing drearily enough in the society of old sea dogs and colonials? That the bonds of sympathy were broken, those mysterious affinities that have at times linked me so closely to all that is beautiful and charming?

I know you will feel for me, for I have more than once seen you plunged in the very same plight. Our two

natures have much in common, and this explains the
tremendous attraction you had for me the first moment
we met. Axiom: It is always one's own self that one
loves in the person of another.

Whenever I come across such an *alter ego,* I am conscious of an accession of strength. It would seem that
the corresponding qualities in two persons combine, and
that sympathy is nothing but a yearning, an impulse,
towards this amalgamation of forces, which, to my mind,
is synonymous with happiness. With your permission
I will call this phenomenon the great sympathetic
paradox.

My language has no literary graces, I know. My
vocabulary is borrowed from dynamics and is utterly
different from that of the best writers, but it expresses
my ideas.

These sympathies manifest themselves in any number
of different ways. What form, I put it to you, do they
take in the case of a musical person like yourself? What
is a sound? Simply a sensation produced in us by a
vibration, which is transmitted by means of the air to
the tympanum and thence to the acoustic nerve. What is
the process within the brain? Let us consider this curious
phenomenon. You are affected by a succession of certain
sounds. You hear a musical phrase, which gives you
pleasure. But why does it give you pleasure? Because
the succession of musical intervals, of which the phrase
consists; in other words, the numerical relations existing
between the different vibrations that proceed from some
resonant body, are expressible by one set of figures rather
than another. Change these figures, and your sympathy
at once ceases to function. You will remark that the
phrase is no longer musical, that it is a mere succession of
incoherent tones. Several sounds are audible simul-
taneously, and you receive an impression, which is
pleasurable or otherwise, by virtue of certain mathe-
matical relations, which form a sympathetic liaison

between an exterior phenomenon and your highly sensitized self. There are genuine affinities between yourself and certain vivid colours, certain effects of light, certain lines, certain forms. Although the relationship established between all these different things and yourself is too complicated to be analyzed, as in the case of music, you are none the less aware that it does exist.

Why is it that we fall in love with one woman rather than another? Often for no better reason than that the oval of her face, the curve of her nose, the arch of her eyebrows—anything that you please—has that indescribable quality, which corresponds to the same mysterious element in ourselves and plays the devil with our imagination. Why protest? Half the time that is all there is to it.

You will tell me that this particular woman possesses a charm of character, a delicacy of feeling, a nobility of mind, which are the true cause of your love. Alas! Beware of ascribing to her that which is essentially your own. Therein lies the origin of all illusions, in this tendency to invest whatever attracts us with qualities, that are to be found nowhere but in ourselves. Thus do we build a shrine for the beloved, and, because he is our friend, mistake an ordinary mortal for a man of genius.

I have been in love with the Venus of Milo and with a nymph of Corregio. The secret of their attraction was certainly neither their conversation nor their intellectual companionship. No, it was a physical affinity, the only kind of love known to the ancients, the only kind of love which has created artists. Nowadays everything has become so complicated that one hardly knows which way to turn. Nine-tenths of mankind have no true comprehension of anything at all.

Granted all this, let us turn, Loti, to its bearing on yourself. There is an affinity between yourself and certain categories of objects. You have, by nature, a tremendous appetite for all artistic and intellectual pleasures, and you can never be content, except in surroundings that stimulate your intense craving for sympathetic reactions. Cut off from these conditions, you cannot expect to be happy. Outside the circumstances which furnish you with this variety of emotion, you will always feel a miserable exile.

A man who is susceptible to these rarefied sensations, which mean nothing to the vast majority of the human race, will be very little moved by anything on a lower plane than his desires. What possible charm can there be in a good dinner, in a day's shooting, in a pretty girl, to a man who has read the poets with tears of ecstasy, who has listened in voluptuous surrender to the lilt of a lovely melody, and has plunged into those reveries that outstrip thought and transcend all speech?

What pleasure is there in watching an endless progression of insipid faces, on which every shade of imbecility is depicted; an unceasing parade of ill-proportioned bodies incarcerated in trousers and black coats, the seething swarms that squirm all over the muddy pavements, right up to the dingy walls, shop fronts and window-boxes. The imagination balks at such a prospect; one's thoughts are petrified at the source.

If your fancy can project itself into the depths of space and time; if you can conceive of an infinity of simultaneous events, occurring all over the surface of the earth, which is itself only a planet revolving round the sun, and the latter merely one focus amongst myriads in space; if you can realise that this simultaneousness, this infinity, is a mere instant in eternity, which is yet another infinity; that all this presents a different aspect, according to the point of view from which you regard it, and that there is an infinity of points of view; if you reflect that the reason of it all, the essence of these things, is hidden from you, and if you vex your spirit with these two eternal problems: What does it all mean? What am I myself in the midst of all these infinities?—Why, then the chances are that you will find no intellectual sympathy between yourself and those who surround you. You will be no more interested in their remarks than if you heard a spider complaining to you that a horrid feather-brush had broken down part of its web, or a toad telling you that it had just fallen heir to a magnificent rubbish heap, in which to dwell at ease. Only to-day an acquaintance thought fit to inform me that he had had a poor harvest, but that someone had left him a house in the country!

So you were in love. Perhaps you have not yet recovered. You thought you had discovered a unique mode of life, a special form of existence, by virtue of which everything was presented to you in a new light.

On these occasions a kind of reaction seems to manifest itself. It is as if a man were born again; for from that moment onwards he lives more intensely and functions more freely. Whatever ideas, whatever emotions he possesses, are revived and stimulated, like the flame in a bowl of punch when you shake it. (Literature of the future!)

He comes out of his shell and is happy. Everything that occurred before the advent of this new joy, vanishes into the night. Hitherto he seems to have been dwelling in a sort of limbo. The past was as utterly different from the glorious present, as a small child's limited existence from that of a young man. The emotional experiences of a lover can only be described at the actual moment of happening. Just now I, personally, am conscious of nothing of the sort. And yet, upon my soul, I have only to dally with these ideas, and immediately I am carried away, with my brain in a whirl and my blood in a fever, till I hardly know whether I am standing on my head or my feet. How good it is to love, to be loved, to know that some rare soul has understood your own, that there is someone who refers her every thought and

act to you, whose nature is as exquisitely subtle as your
own, and who lives, thinks and acts with only you for aim
and object! This it is that makes us strong; this it is
that fosters men of genius.

And then you have the gracious image of your divinity,
not so much a reality, perhaps, as the fine flower of your
imagination; and furthermore that blend of impressions,
physical and mental, sensuous and aesthetic, so utterly
indescribable, which can be recalled only to a mind that
has already experienced them—impressions which, by a
mysterious association of ideas, can be conjured up by
the smallest trifle once owned by the beloved; her very
name, whether you hear it spoken or merely see it written,
and a thousand other divine absurdities besides, which
are perhaps the most precious things this world has to
offer.

Then again you have friendship, a more austere
emotion and more securely based, springing as it does
from that which is best in us, the purely intellectual side
of our nature. What bliss it is to be able to unburden
your mind to someone who can follow your meaning, not
only up to a certain point, but to its furthest conclusion;
someone who completes your thought with the very word
that was trembling on your own lips; someone, whose
answer evokes from you a rush of ideas, a torrent of
conceptions. One little word from your friend means
more to you than a whole string of phrases, for you have
learned to think with him. You understand every
emotion that stirs him, and he is aware of it. You and
he are one in the union of two minds, that are comple-
mentary each to the other.

Surely a man who has known these delights, and is
now bereft of them, is greatly to be pitied.

Ah, me! Here am I without a single bond of affection,
without one soul who cares for me! What is the good
of ideas, if there is no one to whom to impart them?
What is the use of talents, when there is not a person

in the world whose approval I really value? Or of wit, when there is no one to grasp the point?

So one lets everything slide. I have known disillusions enough, yet each day presents some new one. After discovering that nothing in this world endures, that there is absolutely no solid foundation on which to build, one comes to deny everything. The nerves are overwrought; the mind works languidly; one's individuality dwindles, till at times, when one is alone, one wonders if one is asleep or awake. The imagination is paralysed. Farewell to castles in the air! Farewell to hope itself! One takes refuge in cynicism, and talks flippantly of many matters, laughing consumedly—to keep from weeping.

There is nothing for a man to love, who once was ready to love the whole universe. There is nothing for him to believe, though he may still be capable of believing all things. Once he was ready for anything and everything; now he is good for nothing at all.

To feel within one immense potentialities and to know that all are frustrate; to be endowed with the keenest sensibility and to have no object on which to exercise it—what exquisite torture! In such circumstances, life is one long agony, with certain pleasant interludes which afford a momentary respite—witness your circus girl, your odalisque Aziyadé, and your other Turkish enchantresses. But it only ends in one's relapsing again, more bruised than ever.

There you have your confession of faith, expounded, developed and greatly augmented, by the crochetty fellow now writing to you.

The whole point of my long and involved rigmarole is this : I take a very deep interest in you, less perhaps for what you are, than for what I feel you might become. As a counter-irritant to your sorrows, why did you devote yourself to the development of your muscle, destroying in you that which was your one hope of salvation? You have made yourself a clown, an acrobat and a notable marksman. Far better, Loti, have become a great artist!

Another thing. I wanted to instil into you a theory of mine, in which I firmly believe. There is no moral ill without its remedy. It is for us to find it, and to apply it according to the nature of the malady and the temperament of the patient. Despair is an entirely abnormal condition. It is a disease, which can be cured like any other disease. Its natural remedy is time. However unhappy you are, try to keep one little corner of yourself unscathed by this sickness. You will find in it a healing balm. Amen.

Tell me about Stamboul, the Bosphorus, and pashas with three tails.

I kiss the hands of your odalisques.

Ever yours,

PLUNKETT.

XLI

Loti to Plunkett.

Did I tell you, my dear fellow, that I was unhappy? I scarcely think so, and if I did, I was certainly mistaken. Quite the contrary! I came in this evening, convinced that I was one of the lucky people here below, and that the earth itself was a very delectable spot. As I rode home on this lovely January afternoon, the setting sun was gilding the black cypresses, the old crenelated battlements of Stamboul and the roof of my own secluded house, where Aziyadé was waiting for me.

A brazier was warming my room, which was impregnated with the scent of rose essence. After bolting the door, I sat down cross-legged—a more luxurious attitude than you perhaps imagine. My servant Achmet prepared two narghilehs, one for me, one for himself, and placed at my feet a copper tray with a seraglio pastille smouldering on it.

Aziyadé was solemnly crooning the song of the genii and jingling her tambourine. Curls of bluish smoke rose from our narghilehs, and gradually I lost all consciousness of existence, all sense of that woeful human life of ours, as I gazed on the kindly, friendly faces of my three companions: my mistress, my servant and my cat.

In my house there is never an intruder, never an unexpected and unwelcome guest. Now and then a Turk may pay me a discreet visit, when specially invited, but my European friends have not the smallest inkling of my whereabouts, and the ashwood trellisses screen my windows so closely that at no moment of the day can a curious glance penetrate to the interior. The Orientals alone, my dear fellow, really understand the meaning of home. In your European houses, which are open to all comers, you are no more at home than here in the streets. Exposed to the prying of tiresome friends and gossiping neighbours, you have no conception of domestic inviolability or of the charm of such privacy.

Yes, Plunkett, I am happy. I withdraw all the lamentations I was absurd enough to utter. . . . And yet I still feel the ache of all that was broken within my heart. I fear that the present is but a respite, that some sinister fate broods ever over the future and that the bliss of to-day will inevitably bring forth a tragic morrow. Even when she is here with me, I know moments of poignant sadness, like the mysterious agony of mind that used sometimes to seize upon me as a child, with the coming of night.

Yet I am really happy, Plunkett, and feel positively young again. I am no longer the cynical fellow of twenty-seven, who has knocked about so much, seen life, and played the fool in every possible way, in every country under the sun.

Of the three of them, Achmet, Aziyadé and Samuel, it is hard to say which is most a child. They used to make me feel old and disillusioned. In their company, I resembled those characters in Bulwer's book, who lived ten human lives without bearing upon their faces the least sign of age, though within the body of a boy of twenty dwelt an old and battered soul. But now the youthfulness of these three has refreshed my heart. You are right. Perhaps I am still capable of believing all things, I, who had utterly ceased to believe.

XLII

It was a January afternoon. The sky above Stamboul was a leaden grey, and a wintry drizzle was driving before an icy wind. The day was as sunless as a day in England. I was riding along a broad road, which ran on and on between endless walls some twenty feet high, as sheer and smooth and inaccessible as those of a prison. At one particular point, an arched bridge of grey marble, resting on curiously carved marble columns, was swung across the road, connecting the grim masonry on the left and right. Behind the walls lay the Cheraghan Seraglio, with the gardens on one side and on the other the palace and kiosques. The marble bridge enabled the lovely sultanas to pass to and fro without exposing themselves to the public view.

There were only three gates, very far apart, built into the palace ramparts. These gates were of grey marble, and were strengthened with shutters of iron, chased and gilded. The high and imposing portals were suggestive of hidden treasure stored away behind the dreary walls. Each forbidden entrance had its guard of soldiers and black eunuchs. The very architecture of these gates seemed to hint that it was dangerous to cross the threshold; the marble columns and friezes were pierced in the

Arab style and carved all over with strange designs and mysterious scrolls.

A mosque of white marble, topped by a gilded dome and gilded crescents, rose against a background of dark rock, which was mantled with tangled undergrowth. It was as if the wand of some peri had conjured it forth in the twinkling of an eye, in all its snowy whiteness, while purposely preserving the rough and uncouth natural setting.

Three Turkish ladies, complete strangers to me, drove past in a luxurious carriage. One of them, beneath her transparent veil, was evidently endowed with remarkable beauty. Their escort, consisting of two mounted eunuchs, indicated that these ladies were of high rank. Like all Turkish *hanums* of noble family, who think nothing of ogling every European male they see in the streets in the most seductive and challenging manner, these ladies conducted themselves most outrageously. The pretty one in particular smiled at me so winningly that I reined my horse round and followed the carriage. The drive lasted two whole hours and all the time the fair lady sped at me through the open window her most bewitching glances. The carriage bowled swiftly along with myself escorting it, now falling behind, now galloping on ahead. The two eunuchs (the genus is formidable chiefly in comic opera) watched these manœuvres benevolently, and quite unperturbed kept up the same steady trot.

We passed through Dolma Bagche, Sali Bazaar, Top-Hané, the noisy quarter of Galata—then over the Stamboul bridge, and through dreary Phanar and sombre Balat. Finally the carriage drew up in one of the old Turkish streets in Eyoub, in front of an ancient mansion of gloomy but opulent aspect. Here the three ladies got out. Before entering her residence, the fair Seniha (I learnt her name next day) turned round and favoured me with a parting smile. She was charmed at my boldness, and Achmet augured the worst from this adventure.

XLIII

Turkish women, great ladies in particular, make little
account of the fidelity they owe their lords. The severe
surveillance exercised by special male attendants and the
fear of punishment are indispensable as deterrents.
Always idle and bored to distraction, physically oppressed
by the seclusion of the harem, they are ready to throw
themselves at the head of any man they see, the first
servant that comes to hand, or the boatman who rows
them, provided he is handsome and attractive. All of
them are deeply intrigued by young Europeans, who
would doubtless profit by this predilection if they were
aware of it, or if they dared, or if only circumstances
were favourable. My own situation in Stamboul, my
familiarity with the Turkish language and customs, my
solitary door, swinging noiselessly back on its ancient
hinges,—all these advantages would be highly propitious
for such adventures. Had I chosen, I could have made
my house a trysting place for all the languishing beauties
of the harems.

XLIV

A few days later, a black thundercloud bore down upon
my peaceful household, a very terrible thundercloud
indeed, dividing me from her, whom, for all that, I had
never for a moment ceased to love. Aziyadé was up in
arms against a cynical proposal of mine. She resisted
with a strength of will, which strove to master mine, and
this without a tear in her eyes or a quiver in her voice.
I had told her that she need not come the following
evening. Another woman was to take her place for a
day or two. Later, she should return to me and go on
loving me as before, in spite of this humiliation, which
she need not even remember. She was acquainted with
the fair Seniha, who was a byword in all the harems
because of her scandalous intrigues and the impunity
which she enjoyed. Aziyadé detested this creature, at

whom Behijé-hanum was always railing. The idea of
my turning her out to make way for such a wanton overwhelmed her with shame and bitterness.

"I am absolutely determined, Loti," she exclaimed,
"if you ever have that vile Seniha here, all will be over
between us. I shall not even love you. My soul is yours
and all myself. You are free to do as you please. But,
Loti, it will be the end. I may die of grief, but I will
never see you again."

XLV

Yet, such was her love, that within an hour she had
accepted my infamous terms. She left me after promising
to return—later—when that other had departed and it
should please me to send for her.

Aziyadé went away with hot eyes and burning cheeks.
Achmet followed her out of the room, turning round to
inform me that he would never come back. The Arab
draperies over my doorway fell behind them, and I
listened to their slippers trailing across the mats to the
top of the staircase. There the sound ceased. Aziyadé
had collapsed on the steps, and burst into tears. In the
silence of the night I could hear her sobs. Nevertheless,
I did not rush from my room. I let her go.

I had assured her, and it was the truth, that I worshipped her, and her only, and cared nothing at all for
Seniha. It was a mere fever of the senses, which was
sweeping me into the arms of this unknown and intoxicating enchantress. I reflected, in agony of mind, that if
indeed Aziyadé refused to see me again and chose to
barricade herself behind the walls of the harem, she was
lost to me forever. No human power could restore her
to me. With an indescribable pang that clutched at my
heart, I heard the house door close behind her and
Achmet. Then the thought of the fascinating being,
who was to visit me, fired my blood. I stood my ground
and did not call them back.

XLVI

The next evening the whole house was perfumed and bedecked for the reception of this lady of high degree who, in all innocence be it understood, had proposed to honour my solitary abode. Mysteriously, on the stroke of eight, an unheard of hour for Stamboul, the fair Seniha made her appearance. She laid aside her veil and the grey woollen fereja, the humble disguise she had prudently assumed, and revealed herself in a trailing Paris gown, in which she had not the least attraction for me. It was in doubtful taste, costly rather than fashionable, and it did not suit her, as she very soon realised. But although Seniha had missed her mark, she sat down with easy grace, and began to chatter away in a voice devoid of enchantment. Her eyes roamed inquisitively round the room, and she praised its picturesqueness and originality. She kept harping on the strangeness of my way of life and asked me all sorts of indiscreet questions, to which I returned evasive answers.

I gazed at Seniha-hanum. She was really a glorious creature. Her skin had a peachlike bloom; her parted lips were red and dewy. She carried her head thrown back, in the proud consciousness of her sovereign beauty. Voluptuous passion manifested itself in her smile and in the deliberate glances of her dark eyes, veiled by thick lashes.

Seldom had I beheld so lovely a being, close to me, waiting upon my pleasure, in the perfumed warmth of a secret bower. Yet inwardly I was torn by an unexpected conflict. My senses were battling against that vaguer element, which we have agreed to call the soul. My soul was battling against my senses. I felt a burning love for my little darling, whom I had driven away, and my heart was brimming over with tenderness and remorse. The beauty by my side evoked in me repugnance rather than passion. I had desired her. She had come to me. I had only to open my arms. I had asked nothing better—and yet her presence was odious to me.

Conversation languished. An ironic note crept into Seniha's voice. I mastered myself, and with determination, which was proof against this woman's seductions, I turned to her.

" Madame," I said, speaking in Turkish as before, " when, to my infinite regret, you take your departure— and long be it deferred!—may I have the honour of conducting you to your home?"

" I thank you," she replied. " I have an escort."

She was a woman who took no risks. An accommodating eunuch, doubtless accustomed to his mistress's escapades, and prepared for every emergency, was lurking somewhere near my door.

As she crossed the threshold, the great lady burst into mocking laughter, which brought an angry flush to my cheeks. I nearly caught her by her rounded arm and dragged her back. But I controlled myself. After all, I reflected, I had not put myself out for her in the very least, and the laugh was certainly on my side rather than hers.

XLVII

Achmet, who was never coming back, turned up the next morning at eight o'clock. He had mustered an expression of the severest disapproval and coldly bade me good-morning. But my account of Seniha-hanum's visit soon moved him to mirth. Evidently I had, as usual, proved a devil of a fellow (*chok shaitan*), and he retired to a corner to have his laugh out.

Ever afterwards, when in the course of our rides, we passed Seniha in her carriage, the rascal would quiz her with such a suggestive air that I had to take him seriously to task.

XLVIII

despatched Achmet to Oun Capan to see Kadija, and
 inform that monkey-like confidante of my treatment
of Seniha. She was to tell Aziyadé that I implored her
forgiveness and craved her dear presence that very evening. Then I sent children into the country to bring me
branches of verdure and baskets and armfuls of narcissi
and jonquils. The old house was to wear an unwonted
aspect of festivity to welcome her back.

That evening, when Aziyadé entered, she found a
carpet of flowers reaching from the threshold to the door
of our room. The whole floor was deep in fragrant
jonquils, which, stripped from their stalks, diffused an
intoxicating sweetness. The stairs on which her tears
had fallen were completely hidden. Not a word of
comment or reproach escaped from her rosy lips. She
merely smiled, as she looked at the flowers. With her
quick intelligence, she grasped at once the message their
language silently conveyed. Her eyes, ringed with black
from weeping, shone with intense joy. She stepped over
the blossoms, as serene and proud as a little queen entering again upon her lost realm, or like Apsara wandering
over the flowering meads of the Hindoo Paradise. Was
ever houri, or Apsara herself, more lovely, more bloom-
ing, more gracious, more beguiling?

The episode of Seniha-hanum was closed. Its only
result was to make us more devoted to each other than
ever.

XLIX

It was the hour of prayer on a winter's night. The
muezzin was intoning his eternal chant, and we two were
together in our secret retreat at Eyoub. I can still see
her, dear little Aziyadé, very erect and grave, sitting
cross-legged in her Asiatic silk trousers on a pink and blue

Turkish rug—since reft from us by the Jews. She wore that almost mystic expression of hers, which contrasted so strangely with her childlike face and ingenuous mind. She always had this Sibylline look when she was endeavouring to make me follow some argument of hers, which was based as a rule on an oriental parable and therefore absolutely convincing and indisputable.

"*Bak*, Loti," she said, fixing her deep eyes on mine and extending her hand, with outspread fingers. "*Kach tane parmak bourada var?*"

("Look, Loti, how many fingers have I got?")

"Five, Aziyadé," I replied, laughing.

"Yes, Loti, only five. Yet see how different they are! *Bou boundam bir parcha kuchuk.* This one, the thumb, is a little shorter than the next, the second is a little shorter than the third, while this one, the fifth, is the smallest of all."

It was certainly very tiny, Aziyadé's smallest finger. Except for a rim of deep pink at the base, just where it emerged from the skin, the whole nail, like all the others, was stained with henna to a fine deep orange.

"Well, then," she continued, "it is clear that Allah's creatures, who are far more numerous, cannot all be exactly alike—neither the women, nor the men."

The object of this parable was to prove to me, that although other women I had loved could forget me, and other friends deceive me, it was wrong to judge every other man and woman by their example. She, Aziyadé, was not like the others, and would never forget me. Nor would Achmet ever cease to love me.

"So you must stay with us, Loti, stay with us."

She began to picture the future, that dark mysterious future, which always had a fascination for her. There was old age, a far away thing of which she had no very clear idea. Why should we not grow old together, she and I, and go on loving each other to all eternity, in this life and beyond?

" *Sen koja; ben koja.* You will grow old," she said, " and so shall I."

The last phrase was conveyed more by gestures than words. Her young voice rang as if cracked with age; she sat huddled up like a little old woman, her vigorous young body all doubled and bent.

" *Zara yok.* What will it matter, Loti?" she concluded. " We shall still love each other."

L

Eyoub, February 1877.

When you come to think of it, it had a curious beginning, this idyll of ours. Every conceivable blunder and indiscretion was committed day after day, for a month on end, in order to attain a result, which was in itself an utter impossibility.

To wear in the heart of Stamboul a Turkish dress, which to an observant eye erred by its very correctness; in this attire to go wandering through a city, where the simplest question on the part of a passer-by might betray and ruin the rash giaour; to court a Mahommedan lady beneath her balcony, a proceeding without parallel in Turkish annals; and all this, saints above, more for the sake of beguiling the tedious hours and proving one's eccentricity to one's idle comrades; more as a challenge to fate, as an act of bravado, than for love! Strange how success had crowned an enterprise, which was the acme of imprudence, and that by means most calculated to lead to disaster! All this would seem to prove that it is only glaring acts of recklessness that are brought to a happy issue; that fortune favours fools, and that there is a God who protects the rash.

As regards Aziyadé, the first emotions aroused in her heart were curiosity and restlessness. Hence those great eyes of hers, peering through the trellises of the balcony, with astonishment, rather than love, in their gaze. At first she had trembled on behalf of this stranger, who changed his dress, as old Proteus his form, and came in the guise of a gilded Albanian youth to linger beneath her windows.

Later it seemed to her that he must indeed love her deeply, although she was only Aziyadé, the little slave girl, since he risked his life so rashly, merely that he might gaze at her. She never dreamt, poor child, that this youth with the boyish face, was already satiated with all life had to offer, and could bring her nothing, save a disillusioned heart, in quest of some new experience. She thought to herself how good it must be to be loved like that, till gradually she found herself slipping down the slope which led into the arms of a giaour.

She had never been taught a single principle of morality, which might have put her on her guard against herself. Little by little she yielded to the only love poem that had ever been murmured in her ear, and to the terrible fascination of this peril.

And first she had bestowed her hand, through the window bars of the *yali* by the Monastir road; then her arm; then her lips, till one evening she had thrown wide her casement, and, like Marguerite, stolen down into the garden—like Marguerite, all youth and dewy innocence. Even as Marguerite's, her soul was white and virgin, though her childlike body, an old man's purchase, had already lost its purity.

LI

Nowadays, we conduct matters with reasonable security and discretion, thanks to a thorough knowledge of Turkish customs and of every twist and turn of Stamboul. We have become past masters in the art of dissimulation, yet we still come to our trysts in fear and trembling, and we look back on those first months in Salonica as on the memory of some incredible dream. Sitting together by the fire, like a couple of children who

have learnt wisdom and are solemnly shaking their heads
over their past escapades, we talk about those wild times
in Salonica, the sultry, thundery nights, when we roamed
the countryside like a pair of malefactors, or like two
lunatics, drifted over the sea together, unable to interchange a single thought or word. Yet the strangest part
of it all is that I love her. " The azure floweret of a
childlike love," has blossomed again in my heart, by the
grace of her own young and ardent passion. From the
very depths of my soul I love and worship her.

LII

One fine Sunday in January, as I was wandering home
through the cheerful winter sunshine, I saw people with
hand-pumps, and a crowd of onlookers, numbering about
five hundred, in the vicinity of my house.

" What is on fire? " I asked anxiously, for I had
always had a presentiment that some day my house
would be burnt down.

" Make haste, Arif," replied an old Turk, " make
haste. It's your house."

This particular form of emotion was new to me. But
with a brave show of indifference, I approached the little
home which we had vied with each other in adorning,
she for love of me, and I for love of her. A hostile and
menacing crowd made way for me. Angry old beldames
were stirring up the men and railing at me. People had
noticed green flames and a smell of sulphur. I was suspected of sorcery and the black arts. Their original
distrust had only lain dormant, and I was now reaping
the consequences of my enigmatical and disturbing
personality, a stranger without resources and without a
friend to whom to turn.

Slowly I advanced. The doors of the house had been
burst open and all the windows broken; smoke was pouring out through the roof. The whole place had been

overrun and looted by one of those sinister mobs, which spring up in Constantinople at every scene of disorder. I entered the house and received a baptism of charred flakes of plaster, bits of smouldering planking and dirty water mixed with soot. By this time, however, the fire was out. A couple of rooms were gutted, a floor was burnt and two doors and a wall.

By putting a bold front on it I was able to cope with the situation. Bashi-bazouks forced the looters to give up their booty and cleared the square. Two armed zaptiyehs mounted guard at my broken-down door. I left my property to their care, while I ferried across to Galata in the hope of finding Achmet. He was a level-headed fellow and his friendly presence would have been invaluable to me in those critical moments. Within an hour I had reached the heart of that region of taverns and brawls. I looked for him at Madame's and in every other pothouse. But Achmet, that evening, was nowhere to be found. There was nothing for it but to return home, all alone, and to dispose myself to sleep in my room, without door or window to keep out the bitter cold. I rolled myself in wet blankets, which still smelt of burning. My sleep was broken and I was haunted by gloomy thoughts. It was one of the unpleasantest nights I have ever spent.

LIII

The next morning Achmet and I took stock of the damage. It was comparatively slight and could easily be repaired. The burnt out rooms had never been furnished or occupied. If it had been done to order, just for the fun of the thing, the fire could not have been better managed. We recovered all my possessions, down to the smallest trifle. They were blackened and disarranged, but every one of them turned up intact. Achmet developed a feverish activity. He set three old Jewesses to the task of scrubbing and tidying, which led to some ludicrous scenes. By the following day, the whole place had been washed and dried, swept and garnished. Where there had been two rooms, there was now a black and gaping chasm. In every other respect the house was looking itself again, and my room had recovered all its picturesque elegance.

That evening, my apartments were made ready for a great reception. A number of trays were arranged with *rahat-lakoum* (Turkish delight), coffee, and narghilehs, and there was actually an orchestra, consisting of two instruments, a drum and an oboe. It was Achmet who had insisted on this burst of extravagance, and had seen to everything. At seven o'clock I was to receive the authorities and notables, who were to decide my fate, and I awaited my visitors in deep anxiety. I feared I might be obliged to reveal my identity and claim the protection of the British Embassy. Such a result would inevitably lead to orders, cutting short my career in Stamboul, and this solution I dreaded even more than Ottoman justice.

I can still see the whole party, some twenty in all, my landlord, the neighbours, the notables, the judges, the police officers, the dervishes, solemnly seated on my rugs, while the orchestra produced its deafening din and Achmet dispensed brimming cups of coffee and mastic.

They had to consider whether I could clear myself of the charges of arson and witchcraft, and whether I should go to prison, or pay a heavy fine, for having very nearly reduced Eyoub to ashes. Finally there was the question of my landlord's indemnity, and of the repairs to his property, for which I was responsible.

In Turkey everything depends upon one's own exertions, but, as a rule, fortune favours the bold, and assurance is a stepping-stone to success. All that evening I played the great lord, and brazened the matter out, admirably seconded by Achmet, who kept handing round his beverages, and purposely confusing all the different questions and issues. The orchestra continued to rage furiously, and in two hours' time the situation had reached its climax. My visitors were all at cross purposes, and disputing with one another. My case was entirely forgotten.

" There, Loti," said Achmet, " they're all at loggerheads, and it's my doing. You could search all Stamboul and never find a second Achmet. Really, I am invaluable."

The situation was so complicated and so farcical, and Achmet's mirth so infectious, that I yielded to a wild impulse to indulge in acrobatics. Suddenly, without warning, I dropped down on my hands and executed two cartwheels, one after the other, before the eyes of the bewildered audience. In ecstasies over this performance, Achmet turned the diversion to account. Bowing profusely, he presented each visitor with his pattens, cloak and lantern, and the meeting broke up without having arrived at any decision.

In the end, I did not go to prison, nor did I pay a fine. My landlord had the house repaired at his own expense, blessing Allah the while for having spared the other half. I still remained the spoilt child of the neighbourhood.

Two days later, Aziyadé returned to find the house just as before, in perfect order and full of flowers.

How the fire could break out, all by itself, in a locked-up house, is a baffling mystery, which has never been solved.

LIV

" Whoso swimmeth in the Ocean of Love,
The waves shall cast him on the shores of Oblivion.
Whoso seeketh his heart's desire
Shall find Annihilation where he sought Repose,
And in the end discover naught but Nothingness."
(FERIDEDDIN ATTAR, Persian Poet.)

Izeddin-Ali-Effendi was holding a reception in his house, which was situated in the heart of Stamboul. The fumes of incense mingled with the smoke of *tembaki*, and the coppery jingling of tambourines blended with male voices, dreamily chanting strange Eastern melodies. These entertainments, which at first struck me as utterly weird and barbaric, have gradually lost their strangeness. I sometimes give similar parties myself, at which guests are welcomed with the same intoxicating perfumes, while the tambourines rattle about their ears. Izeddin-Ali's guests arrive at nightfall and never leave till daylight. On snowy nights, the distances in Stamboul are a serious consideration, and Izeddin is the soul of hospitality. Outwardly, his house is old and shabby, but its sombre walls enshrine all the mysterious sumptuousness of Oriental luxury. Izeddin-Ali professes the cult of everything that is *eski*, everything that recalls the good old days and is stamped with the seal of the past.

You knock at the heavy ironbound door, which is noiselessly opened by two small Circassian slaves. You put out your lantern and remove your shoes, two homely rites required by Turkish custom. The Oriental home is never defiled with mud from the streets; the precious carpets, handed down from father to son, are trodden only by the babouche or the bare foot.

The small slave-girls are not more than eight years old and are for sale, as they are aware. They are enchanting, with their beaming smiles and regular features; flowers deck the baby locks, which are piled high on their heads. Respectfully they take the visitor's hand and gently raise it to their forehead. Aziyadé, who was once a little Circassian slave herself, still has a way of expressing her love and her submission with this gesture.

As you ascend the dark stairs, which are covered with sumptuous Persian carpets, the haremlik is quietly unlatched, and through a half-opened door, encrusted with mother-of-pearl, bright eyes survey you. In a great hall, covered with rugs so thick that you seem to be walking on the fleecy back of a Cashmere ram, five or six young

men are seated cross-legged in postures of calm beatitude
and peaceful reverie. A huge brazier of chased copper
diffuses a pleasant, if somewhat heavy, warmth, which
induces drowsiness.

From the carved oaken ceiling hang clusters of candles,
enclosed in opalescent globes, which shed a rosy light,
dim and discreet. No women are present. In place of
chairs, which are conspicuous by their absence, there are
low divans, covered with rich Asiatic silks, and cushions
of brocade and gold embroidered satin. Silver trays are
set out with long chibouks of jasmine, and there are little
stands with eight flaps, holding narghilehs, which are
finished off with big amber balls encrusted with gold.

Not everyone is received into Izeddin-Ali's house. His
guests are carefully chosen, not from the degenerate
coxcombs, the pashas' sons, who have loafed about on
the boulevards of Paris, but from the scions of ancient
Turkey, who have been reared in gilded yalis, sheltered
from the levelling blasts, which, fraught with the reek
of coal smoke, are blowing from the West. In all this
company you will see none but prepossessing faces, and
eyes radiant with youthful ardour. These men, who go
about in European dress during the daytime, resume in
the evening, in the inviolable sanctuary of the home, the
silken tunic and the long fur-lined cashmir caftan. The
grey overcoat is merely a temporary disguise, an un-
attractive garment quite unsuited to the Asiatic temperament.

Curls of fragrant smoke, continually twisting and
changing, rise in the warm air. Voices are hushed. The
principal topics of conversation are the war, Ignatieff, the
alarming Muscovites, and the tragic fate with which
Allah is threatening the Khalif and all Islam. The tiny
cups are frequently replenished with Arabian coffee. The
ladies of the harem, only too delighted to be in evidence,
glide in and out through the half-open door, bearing the
silver trays in their own fair hands. A glimpse of finger-

tips, of bright eyes, of an arm, hastily withdrawn! Nothing more. At ten o'clock, the fifth hour by Turkish reckoning, the door of the haremlik is closed and the ladies do not re-appear.

A loving-cup, filled with the white wine of Ismidt, which the Koran does not forbid, is passed round and everyone drinks of it, according to custom. The little sip you take would hardly content a girl; so the wine can have little to do with the supervening langour.

Gradually heads begin to nod and through the mind drift the haziest ideas, blended together in a vague dream. Both Izeddin-Ali and Suleiman take up a tambourine and croon, in the voice of somnabulists, old airs of Asia. Dimmer and dimmer grow the spires of smoke, the drooping eyelids, the gleaming mother-of-pearl, the whole sumptuous room, till softly there ensues the intoxication, the oblivion, desired by all human creatures. Servants come in with yatags and everyone lies down to sleep. . . .

It is morning. The light filters in through ashwood trellises, painted blinds and silken curtains. Each guest retires to a white marble dressing-room, provided with towels so richly embroidered with gold that in England one would hardly dare to touch them. After smoking a cigarette round the copper brazier, the party breaks up.

The awakening brings disenchantment. It was only a dream from the Arabian nights, you feel, when you find yourself floundering through the mud in the busy streets and marts of Stamboul.

LV

All the nocturnal noises of Constantinople linger in my memory, blended with her murmured explanations of many a strange thing. The most sinister sound of all was the voice of the *beckjüs,* the night watchmen, uttering the terrible shout of *Yangun Var* (Fire!), a prolonged wailing cry, echoed in every quarter of Stamboul, through the deathlike silence. Towards morning began the mellow crowing of cocks, heralding the dawn, to be followed a few minutes later by the prayer of the muezzins, which for us was fraught with melancholy, since it ushered in another day, with its torturing uncertainty in all that concerned my love, her return to me at evening, and her very life itself.

One of the first nights she spent with me in the lonely house at Eyoub, we heard, quite close to us, on the old staircase, a sound which struck terror to our hearts. We fancied, both of us, that a troop of genii, or of turbaned men with daggers and naked yataghans, were creeping up the worm-eaten steps to our door. When we were together, she and I, we had everything to fear. Small wonder if we trembled ! But presently the noise was repeated, and this time it was more distinct and less alarming; in fact, its origin could no longer be questioned.

" *Sechan!* " (Mice!), laughed Aziyadé, completely reassured.

The old tumbledown house was full of them, and at night they fought among themselves pitched battles of the most murderous description.

" *Chok sechan var senin evdé,* Loti ! " she would say. " What a lot of mice there are in your house ! "

So one fine evening she presented me with young Kedi-bey, his lordship the cat.

Kedi-bey, who eventually grew into a magnificent big Tom, was then barely a month old, a tiny ball of yellow fluff with great green eyes, and already a terrible glutton. She brought him, as a surprise for me, in one of those gold-embroidered velvet satchels, in which Turkish children carry their schoolbooks. She had had it ever since the days, when, a bare-legged child, without a veil, she used to go for most inadequate instruction to the old turbaned schoolmaster in the village of Canlija, on the Asiatic shores of the Bosphorus. She had profited but little by his lessons, and could hardly write. But she was very fond of this poor, old, faded satchel, the companion of her earliest childhood. Kedi-bey was presented to me wrapped up in a silken napkin. Round his neck was a collar, which Aziyadé had painstakingly embroidered in gold. He looked so quaint and so tousled, when she unpacked him, that Achmet and I were convulsed with laughter.

Never, as long as I live, shall I forget my first introduction to Kedi-Bey.

LVI

Allah, Mah Allah, ve Mohammed resul Allah. Allah *is* God and Mahomet is His prophet!

Day after day, from time immemorial, at the selfsame hour, to the self-same chant, that cry has rung out from the top of the minaret across this old house of mine. Intoned in the muezzin's shrill voice, it has been wafted to the four corners of the earth with a mechanical regularity, a fatal inevitableness. Some, who are now only a handful of ashes, heard it, as we hear it, who are but of yesterday. For three hundred years, without one lapse, in dim winter dawns, as at glorious sunrises, the sacred watchword of Islam has echoed through the vibrant morning air, mingled with the crowing of cocks and the first sounds of awakening life. A melancholy reveillé, breaking in upon our sleepless nights of love!

It is time to part, to snatch a hasty farewell, in the dread that we may never meet again. That very day, perhaps, some sudden betrayal, some swift vengeance on the part of an old man, betrayed by his four wives, may sunder us forever. That very day may come to pass one of those dark tragedies of the harem, against which human justice is powerless, and all material help of no avail.

Away she goes, dear little Aziyadé, muffled like a woman of the people in a coarse grey woollen gown, fashioned for her here in my house. Her graceful body bent, she hobbles along on a stick, her face hidden by a thick yashmak.

Her caïque deposits her in the busy quarter of the bazaars. At Kadija's house, she resumes the dress of a cadi's lady and in broad daylight returns to her master's harem. For the sake of appearances, she brings back from her expedition some trifle, such as a flower or ribbon, to imply that she has been shopping.

LVII

Achmet was full of gravity and importance. The two of us were bound on a mysterious expedition. But whereas he was primed with Aziyadé's instructions, I had promised to go whither I was led and to do as I was told. At the Eyoub jetty, Achmet haggled over a caïque to take us to Azar-Kapou. The bargain concluded, he told me to get in.

" Sit down, Loti," he said solemnly, and we pushed off.

At Azar-Kapou I had to follow him through the vilest slums, squalid, filthy, dark and sinister, populated by vendors of tar, and old pulleys and rabbit skins. We went from door to door, asking for old Dimitraki, whom we found at last, lurking in a loathsome hovel. He was an aged Greek, all in rags, and, despite his white beard, he looked a regular brigand.

Achmet handed him a paper with Aziyadé's name scrawled on it, whereupon he made a long speech, which I could not follow, in the language of Homer. The old ruffian then produced from the depths of a filthy chest a bundle of tiny stylets. From these he selected the sharpest, a preliminary by no means calculated to re-assure me. My recollection of the classics enabled me to understand his next remark.

" Show me the place," he said, turning to Achmet.

Achmet opened my shirt and put his finger on the left
side of my chest, just above the heart.

LVIII

The operation was completed without much pain.
Achmet presented the artist with a ten-piastre note, out
of Aziyadé's own purse.   Old Dimitraki exercised the
curious profession of tattooer to the Greek sailors.   He
was remarkable for his accuracy and lightness of touch.
I came away with a little, sore, red patch on my chest,
made by countless tiny scratches, which, as soon as they
healed, would reproduce in a fine shade of blue Aziyadé's
name in Turkish.   According to Mussulman belief, this
tattooing, like every other mark or blemish upon my
earthly body, would accompany me into eternity.

LIX

Loti to Plunkett.

_____

February 1877.

What a glorious night it was!   Oh, Plunkett, the
beauty of Stamboul!   At eight that evening I had left
the *Deerhound*.   After a long walk, I reached Galata,
looked in at Madame's to call for my friend Achmet,
and the two of us made our way through the deserted
Mussulman quarters to Azar-Kapou.   Every evening
we had the choice of two routes from Azar-Kapou to
Eyoub.   The one led across the great bridge of boats
to Stamboul, and thence by footpaths through Phanar,
Balat and the cemeteries; it was direct and picturesque,
but at night beset with dangers, and we never undertook
it unless our trusty Samuel was there to make a third.

That evening we hired a caïque at the bridge of Kara-Keui, and proceeded peacefully home by sea.

There was not a breath of wind, not a sound, not a ripple on the water. Stamboul lay wrapt in a vast winding sheet of snow. In that city of sun and azure sky the effect was incongruously arctic, as well as strangely impressive. The hills, sprinkled with thousands of sombre houses, glided past us, all merged together that evening beneath one smooth, unbroken pall of eerie white. Above those human ant heaps, buried deep in snow, rose the grandiose, grey masses of the mosques and the tapering spires of the minarets. Through a veil of mist, the moon bathed the entire landscape in a wan, bluish radiance.

On reaching Eyoub, we saw a shaft of light filtering through the trellises and the thick window curtains. She was there already—the first to arrive at the trysting place.

You see, Plunkett, you with your European houses, which are so tiresomely accessible both to the owners and others, can have no idea of the bliss of such homecoming, which in itself is worth all the dangers and difficulties.

LX

There will come a day, when of all this dream of love, nothing will remain; when, together with ourselves, all will be swallowed up in darkest night, even to the names on our tombstones.

There is a country which I love and long to visit: Circassia with its gloomy mountains and mighty forests. It has for me a fascination, which emanates from Aziyadé. It is from this country that she draws her life's blood and the breath of her body. When I watch the fierce, half-savage Circassians pass by, wrapped in pelts, I feel a secret attraction towards these strangers, who are of the same blood as my beloved.

Aziyadé herself can remember a great lake, on the banks of which she thinks she was born; a village lost in the depths of a forest, of which she has forgotten the name, and a stretch of shore where she played in the open air with the other little children of that race of mountaineers.

What lover does not yearn to wrest from the past the lost years of his mistress? He would fain have seen her face in childhood and at every stage of her development; petted the tiny girl and watched her grow up, with no arms save his own to enfold her, with no one to cheat him of her kisses, with no one but himself to own her, love her, touch her, gaze at her. Jealous of her past, he grudges everything that, before his coming, she gave to others, the slightest emotion of her heart, the least little word from her lips that fell on other ears. The present does not suffice; he covets all her past and all her future. Hand clasps hand; heart beats on heart, lips are pressed to lips. Yet he yearns for a more exquisite sensitiveness, a more perfect union, welding them together and making them utterly one.

" Aziyadé," I say, " tell me more about your childhood and the old schoolmaster at Canlija."

Aziyadé smiles and ransacks her brain for some fresh tale, with which she interweaves her own original comments and quaint asides. Her favourite stories, in which the hojas (sorcerers) play the chief part, are always the oldest of all, stories which have nearly faded from her mind and are hardly more than shadowy memories of her infancy.

" It's your turn now, Loti," she says presently. " Go on where you left off; you were just sixteen."

Alas! there is nothing I can tell her in the language of Chengiz, that I have not already told others in many another tongue. Everything she says to me, others have said to me before. All these words, so inconsequent, so deliciously absurd, other lips have already whispered, almost inaudibly in my ear. The charm of other women, whose very memory has faded from my heart, has cast over other countries, other haunts, and other dwellings, a glamour which has passed away. I have shared with another woman this same dream of eternal love. We swore to worship each other here on earth, one in heart and soul, as long as there was life in our veins, and then to sleep together in one grave. The same earth should take us to her bosom and our dust be mingled to all eternity. Yet all that is over and done with, blotted out and swept away. Young though I am, I have already forgotten. If there is a hereafter, who will be my companion in the new life, she or you, my little Aziyadé?

Among all these mysterious ecstasies, these consuming raptures, who shall distinguish that which is of the senses, from that which is of the heart? Is it the soul's supreme impulse towards heaven, or the blind prompting of nature, seeking to recreate and renew itself? Unanswerable questions, which all mortal men have put to themselves, so that it is idle to ask them yet again. We are ready to believe in a spiritual and eternal union, because we love each other. But how many thousands before us have thus believed, how many thousands have loved, down through the ages, and, in that radiant hope, fallen trustfully asleep, beguiled by the mocking mirage of death? Alas! in twenty years, ten years even, where shall we be, poor little Aziyadé, you and I? Laid in the earth, two handfuls of forgotten dust, our very graves perhaps hundreds of miles apart. Who will ever remember that we loved each other? The time will come when of our dream of love nothing will remain, when we twain shall be lost in darkest night, and no trace of us survive, not even the names upon our tombs.

Still will the little Circassian slave girls leave the mountains for the harems of Constantinople; still will the dreary chant of the muezzin ring out through the silent winter mornings. But us it will never wake again.

LXI

The question of my journey to Angora, the cats' capital, had long been in debate. At last I was granted ten days' leave on condition that I undertook not to get into any trouble in those parts, which would necessitate the intervention of my Embassy.

My fellow-travellers and I assembled at Scutari in cloudless weather. The party included two dervishes, Riza-effendi and Mahmoud-effendi, several of my Stamboul friends, some Turkish ladies, some servants, and a large quantity of baggage. This picturesque caravan moved off in broad sunshine, down the long avenue of cypresses, which cuts across the great cemeteries of Scutari. The spot has a funereal majesty and these heights command an incomparable view of Stamboul.

LXII

The deeper we plunge into the mountains, the more does the snow retard our progress. There is no possibility of our reaching Angora under a fortnight. After a three-days' march, I decide to take leave of my travelling companions. Achmet and I, suitably mounted, turn our horses' heads southwards, with the idea of visiting Nicomedia and Nicaea, those two notable cities of Christian antiquity.

Of this first part of our journey, my memory records a wild, well-wooded country, with cool fountains, with deep valleys, mantled with green oaks, spindle-trees and flowering rhododendrons. All this in glorious winter weather, under a light powering of snow.

We put up in the various *hane*, hovels of indescribable squalor, of which the one at Mudurlu is perhaps the most characteristic specimen. Arriving at Mudurlu at night-fall, we made our way into a large, dark room on the first floor of an old, smoke-blackened *hane,* where a motley crew of gipsies and bearleaders was already sleeping. The ceiling was so low that we could not stand upright. The fare consisted of one enormous stewpot, with dubious looking lumps floating about in a thick gravy. This dish was placed on the ground and the whole company gathered round it. A single napkin, literally several yards long, was handed round, and used by each person in turn.

Achmet declared he would rather die of cold outside, than sleep in this filthy den. But within an hour, the two of us, who came in chilled to the bone and utterly worn out, were lying there fast asleep.

We rose before dawn, and with the wind blowing full upon us, washed from head to foot in the crystal waters of a fountain.

LXIII

At dusk the next evening we reached Ismidt (Nicomedia). Here we were arrested for travelling without passports. A certain pasha, however, obligingly came to the rescue with two fanciful documents of his own composition. After prolonged negotiations we managed to avoid having to sleep in the lockup. Our horses, however, were put into the pound for the night.

Ismidt is a large and sufficiently civilised Turkish town, situated on a splendid bay, and its bazaars are busy as well as picturesque. The inhabitants are forbidden to be abroad after eight in the evening, with or without lanterns.

I still cherish the memory of our morning at Ismidt. Spring was in the air and the sun already warm in a clear blue sky. Our papers were in order and we ourselves fit and hearty. After a rough but substantial breakfast, we set out to climb Orkhanjami. We scrambled up the narrow streets, overgrown with weeds and as steep as goat tracks. Butterflies were fluttering, insects humming, birds singing of spring, and a soft breeze blowing. The quaint, old, tumbledown houses were painted with flowers and arabesques. On every roof, storks were building their nests with such utter indifference to the affairs of others, that their operations sometimes blocked up the windows entirely.

From the top of Orkhanjami the sight ranges over the azure Gulf of Ismidt and the rich plains of Asia Minor to the Olympus of Brussa, in the far distance, with its lofty snow-capped peak soaring into the sky.

LXIV

From Ismidt we proceeded to Tau-chanjil and thence to Kara-Musar in the rain. From Kara-Musar we rode to Nicaea through gloomy mountain scenery under a fall of snow. Winter had returned. This stage of our journey was not without incident. One Ismael, accompanied by three zeibeks armed to the teeth, proposed to strip us, but, thanks to the unexpected appearance of some bashi-bazouks, the situation was saved and we arrived at Nicaea, muddy but unharmed. Here I confidently presented my passport, the fabrication of the Pasha at Ismidt, in which I figured as a Turkish subject. In spite of my still rather halting Turkish, the authorities were taken in by my costume and my rosary. So here I am, a real authentic effendi!

At Nicaea there are ancient Christian shrines, dating from the first centuries of the Christian era, among them a St. Sophia (Aya Sophia), which is the elder sister to the earliest churches of Western Europe. Here we had more bearleaders for bedfellows. Our original intention was to make our way back by Brussa and Mudania, but as we were running short of money, we returned to Kara-Musar, where we spent our last piastres on breakfast.

After discussing the situation, I handed over my shirt to Achmet, who went off to sell it. The proceeds were sufficient for the return journey and we embarked with hearts as light as our purses.

We were delighted to see Stamboul reappear. These few days had transformed the entire aspect of nature. New plants were sprouting on my terraced roof. A litter of puppies, which first saw the light of day on my doorstep, were beginning to yap and wag their tails. Their mother gave us a great welcome.

LXV

The evening brought Aziyadé, full of the anxiety she had endured on my behalf and the countless times she had exclaimed :

" *Allah! Selamet versen Loti!* " (Allah, protect Loti !)

From the folds of her gown, where it had been carefully hidden, she produced a tiny box, smelling of rosewater like everything of hers. Inside, there was something small and heavy. Beaming with joy, she laid this mysterious object in my hand.

" Look, Loti, here's a present for you."

It was a solid ring of hammered gold, with her name engraved upon it. For a long time it had been a dream of hers to give me a ring with her name on it, so that I could take it away with me to my own country. But the poor child had no money. She lived in great comfort, almost in luxury. She was able to transfer from her house to mine strips of embroidered silk, cushions and other objects, of which she could dispose as she pleased. But she was given very little money. All payments were at the discretion of her maid, Emineh, and she could hardly save out of her meagre pocket-money enough to buy a ring. Then she thought of her own jewellery. She dared not send it to the goldsmiths' bazaar to be bartered or sold; so she hit on another plan. She gave all her trinkets to be crushed under the hammer of a Scutari smith, who was pledged to secrecy, and she brought them to me to-day in the shape of this great, rough, massive ring of gold. At her desire, I swore never to lay it aside, but to wear it to the end of my days.

LXVI

It was a glorious morning in winter—that mild winter of the Levant. Aziyadé had left Eyoub an hour before us, and clad in a robe of grey, had made her way down the Golden Horn. Now, all in pink, she was proceeding upstream to rejoin her master's harem at Mehmed-Fatih. She looked smiling and gay beneath her white veil. Old Kadija was seated beside her, the two of them comfortably settled in the bottom of a slender caïque, of which the bows were decorated with beading and gilding.

Achmet and I, who were bound in the opposite direction, were lying on the red cushions of a long caïque, rowed by two boatmen.

Constantinople lay steeped in the glory of morning. Palaces and mosques, still with the rose of sunrise upon them, were mirrored in the calm depths of the Golden Horn. Flocks of black divers (*karabataks*) were performing the quaintest antics around the fishing boats, and plunging head first into the cold, blue waters.

Chance, or our caïqjis' humour, brought our two gilded barques so close that the oars were intermingled. The boatmen paused to exchange the customary insults.

"Dog! Son of a dog! Great-grandson of a dog!"

Kadija ventured to steal a smile at us, her long white teeth flashing between her black lips. But Aziyadé passed us without a quiver of the eyelids. She seemed absorbed in the frolics of the *karabataks*.

"Look at that wicked old bird!" she said to Kadija.

LXVII

" When the season of delight is over, who can say which of us
    will still be left in the land of the living?
Let us be merry while we may, for spring is swift of foot and
    will not linger.
List to the song of the nightingale : Spring is coming.
In every thicket, spring has quickened the fountain of joy.
The almond tree is decked with silvery blossom.
Be merry; be joyful; for spring is fleet of foot, and will not
    linger."

                                            —(*Old Oriental Poem.*)

Spring is here again; the almond trees are in flower.
And I, I contemplate with horror each new season, which
hurries me on towards the night, each new year which
brings me nearer to the abyss.   Whither am I going, my
God?   What lies beyond?   Who will be by my side, when
the dark cup is held to my lips?

" It is the season of joy and pleasure.   Spring is here.
Spare me your prayers, sir priest.   Your time will come."

IV

I

Stamboul, March 19th, 1877.

The orders recalling the *Deerhound* to Southampton came like a bolt from the blue. I moved heaven and earth to evade them and to prolong my stay at Constantinople. I knocked at every door, even at that of the Ottoman army, which was very nearly opened to me.

" My dear fellow," said the pasha in excellent English and with the exquisite courtesy of the well-bred Turk, " My dear fellow, do you propose at the same time to embrace the faith of Islam? "

" No, Excellency," I replied, " I should have no objection to becoming a naturalised Ottoman and to changing my name and country, but officially I should remain a Christian."

" All the better," he replied, " I approve. Mahommedanism is not an indispensable condition, and we have no liking for renegades. But I think I may warn you that your services could not be accepted as a temporary measure, and that, in any case. your Government would certainly raise objections. But your offer might be considered on a permanent basis. Ask yourself whether you wish to throw in your lot with us. I hardly see how you could avoid sailing with your ship; there is scarcely time to arrange matters. Besides, your absence would give you time to think it all over, before coming to such a serious decision, and you could still come back to

140

us later on. But if you prefer it, I can lay your request before His Majesty the Sultan this evening, and I have every reason to believe that his answer would be favourable."

"Excellency," I replied, "if possible I should like to have the matter settled immediately. Later on you will have forgotten me. Only, I should have to apply for leave at once, to go and see my mother."

I stipulated, however, for one hour's grace, and went away to think it over.

My hour was all too short; the minutes seemed like moments. My mind was confused with a feverish rush of thoughts. I wandered at random through the streets of the old Mussulman quarter, which spreads over the heights of Taxim, between Pera and Funducli. The weather was gloomy and sultry. The old wooden houses were of every shade of colour, from black and dark grey to reddish brown. Turkish women, swathed to the eyes in scarlet or orange silks embroidered with gold, tripped along the dry pavements in their little yellow slippers. Long, sloping vistas revealed glimpses of the white Seraglio with its groves of black cypresses, of Scutari and the Bosphorus, half veiled in blue mist. To renounce name and country is a more serious matter than one imagines, when it presents itself as a real and urgent question, to be settled, once and for all, in the space of one short hour.

Once rivetted to Stamboul for life, should I still retain my affection for it? England itself, the monotonous routine of British domestic life, friends, both tedious and ungrateful, I can relinquish without a pang of regret or remorse. I embrace this new country in a moment of supreme crisis. This spring, the war will decide its fate, and with it, my own. As the Yuzbashi Arif, I shall be entitled to as much leave as I am now in the British Navy, and I shall still be able to visit my dear ones at home, under the old lime trees at Brightbury.

Heavens above, why not? A Yuzbashi, a Turk, for good and all, and able to remain with her! I pictured the rapturous moment, when I should return to Eyoub in the dress of a Yuzbashi, and tell her that I would never leave her again.

At the end of the hour, my decision was irrevocably made. It would break my heart to go away and desert her. I sought another interview with the pasha, with the firm intention of pronouncing the solemn assent, which would link me to Turkey forever. I would beg him to present my petition to the Sultan that very evening.

II

As soon as I entered the pasha's presence I felt myself trembling. There was a mist before my eyes.

"Excellency," I said, "I thank you, but I cannot accept your proposal. Yet I entreat you not to forget me. When I am in England I may write to you." . . .

III

It was high time to think of my departure. In the evening I went all over Pera, leaving P.P.C. cards, but without waiting to be received. Achmet, in ceremonial attire, walked behind me carrying my overcoat.

"Ah, Loti," he said at last, " you are going to leave us; you are paying your farewell visits. I have guessed it, you see. Now, if you really care for us and are bored by these people, if you set no store by their conventions, why do you bother about them? Take off those ugly black clothes and that absurd hat, and come with me to Stamboul as fast as you can. Let the others go hang."

The result of Achmet's protest was that several of my calls remained unpaid.

IV

Stamboul, March 20th, 1877.

One final drive with Samuel! Each of our minutes is numbered. Inexorable time is sweeping away these last hours, wintry, grey and cold, with the sudden squalls of March. And then comes the moment that we must part forever. We agreed that Samuel should take ship for his own country, before my own departure for England. As a last favour, he begged me to take a drive with him in an open carriage, until he heard the warning whistle of his steamer. That fellow Achmet, who had supplanted him, and was to follow me to England some day, added to his grief. He was sick with sorrow, and could not understand, poor lad, that there was all the difference in the world between his own agonising love for me and Mihran-Achmet's pure and brotherly affection. He could not realise that he was a hothouse plant, which could never be transferred to my placid home in England.

The *arabahji* urges his horses to a rapid trot. Samuel looks like a pasha, arrayed in my fur coat with which I have presented him. His handsome face is pale and sad. Silently he contemplates the different quarters of Stamboul, as they glide past; the great, empty squares, overgrown with grass and moss; the towering minarets and old, tumbledown mosques, standing out white against a leaden sky; all the venerable buildings with the stamp of age and decay upon them, and falling to ruins, like Islam itself.

Swept by the last gusts of winter, Stamboul lies desolate and forlorn. The muezzins are chanting the evening prayer. The moment of departure is at hand. I had grown fond of my poor Samuel, and I promised him, as one promises a child, that for his sake, too, I would come back again. I would visit Salonica on purpose to see him. But he knows that we shall never meet again, and his tears go to my heart.

V

March 21st.

Poor dear little Aziyadé! I had not the courage to say to the child herself:

"I am going away the day after to-morrow."

It was evening when I returned to my house. The setting sun was flooding my room with its glorious crimson rays. Spring was in the air. The cafejis had set their tables out-of-doors, as if the summer had come. All my neighbours were sitting in the street, smoking their narghilehs under almond trees snowy with blossom.

Achmet shared the secret of my approaching departure. The two of us made desperate efforts at conversation. But Aziyadé had begun to suspect, and scanned our faces with great questioning eyes. Nightfall found the three of us as silent as the dead.

At seven in the evening, the first hour by Turkish reckoning, Achmet brought in an old packing case, which, turned upside down, served us for table. On this he laid our meagre supper. Previous transactions with Isaac the Jew had reduced us to our last farthing. As a rule our tête-à-tête dinner was a merry meal, and we used to laugh at our own destitution. Here were we two, who went clad in silk and gold and reclined on Turkish carpets, munching dry bread off an old packing case!

Aziyadé followed my example and sat down. But her plate remained untouched. Her eyes were fixed on my face with strange intentness. We dreaded, both of us, to break the silence.

"Come, Loti," she said at last. "I understand. This is the end. Tell me the truth."

Her tears began to rain down upon her crust of dry bread.

"No, Aziyade. No, my love," I cried. "We have still to-morrow. I swear it. But after that, . . . I cannot tell. . . ."

Achmet saw that supper was spread in vain. Without a word, he removed the old packing case and the earthenware plates, and left us alone in the gathering darkness.

VI

The next day we were confronted with the task of stripping and dismantling our dear little home, furnished bit by bit and with such loving care, that each separate object evoked some memory of its own. Two *hamals* (porters), engaged for this purpose, were awaiting my orders to set to work. It occurred to me to send them away to their dinner and thus postpone for a while the work of destruction.

"Loti," said Achmet, "why not make a drawing of your room? In days to come, when you are old and grey, you will look at it and remember us."

And so I spent my hour of grace making a drawing of my Turkish room. The years will be hard put to it to efface the charm of those memories.

When Aziyadé arrived, she found the walls bare and the whole place in disorder. It was the beginning of the end. Nothing but packing-cases and bundles, and general confusion. The surroundings she had loved so much, had vanished forever. The white mats which covered the floor, the carpets on which our bare feet had trodden, had all been sent to the Jews. Everything had resumed its old look of sordid misery.

Aziyadé entered almost gaily. She had strung herself up, I hardly know how. But the sight of that desolate room was too much for her. She burst into tears.

K

VII

Like a condemned prisoner asking a final boon, she besought me to do everything she asked of me on our one remaining day.

"To-day, Loti," she said, "you must not say no to anything. You are not to disapprove. You must agree to whatever comes into my head."

Returning from Galata by caïque, about nine that evening, I heard, proceeding from my house, the unusual strains of singing and primitive music. In one of the rooms, which had recently been burnt out, in the midst of a cloud of dust, I saw a chain of dancers, executing one of those Turkish dances, which terminate only with the complete exhaustion of the performers. A motley crew of Greek and Mussulman sailors, picked up on the quays of the Golden Horn, were dancing furiously, and refreshing themselves with raki, mastic and coffee.

Our household friends, Suleiman, old Riza and the dervishes Hassan and Mahmud, looked on at this spectacle in utter amazement.

The music issued from my room, where I found Aziyadé herself turning the handle of one of those great, deafening, Levantine barrel organs, which grind out Turkish dance tunes in shrieking tones, to the tinkling accompaniment of Chinese bells.

Aziyadé had laid aside her veil, and through the half-open door, the dancers could see her face. This was not only contrary to all custom, but to the most elementary ideas of prudence. Never before in that holy quarter of Eyoub had such a scandalous scene been enacted. Had not Achmet declared to all who were present, that she was an Armenian, she must have been lost. Achmet was sitting in a corner, resigned and acquiescent. The affair was comical, and, at the same time, harrowing. I could hardly restrain my laughter, yet the look on her face wrung my heart. These little girls, fatherless and

motherless, reared in the shadow of the harem, may well
be forgiven their outrageous notions.   Their actions
cannot be judged by the laws that govern Christian
women.   She was frantically turning the handle of the
barrel organ and extorting from this huge musical box
excruciating sounds.   Turkish music has been defined as
convulsions of devastating gaiety, and that evening the
truth of this paradoxical utterance was brought home to
me.

Before long she grew alarmed at her own behaviour,
and at the noise she was making.   Deeply ashamed, she
realised that she was unveiled in full view of all those
men.   She ordered the organ grinder to resume his task,
while she withdrew to a large divan, the one remaining
piece of furniture in the house, and asked for a cigarette
and a cup of coffee.

VIII

Aziyadé's Turkish coffee was brought to her in the
usual tiny cup, half the size of an egg-shell, of the customary blue, with a copper base.   She seemed calmer
now and looked at me with a smile.   Her limpid, sorrowful eyes asked my pardon for all that rabble and uproar.
Like a petted child, aware that it has been in mischief,
she pleaded with eyes more charming and persuasive than
any spoken eloquence.   The dress she wore that evening
invested her with strange beauty.   The oriental richness
of her attire contrasted with the present aspect of the
house, which had lapsed once more into its former squalid
dreariness.   She wore one of those flowing tunics with
long basques, of which the Turkish women of to-day
have almost lost the pattern.   It was of violet silk,
embroidered with golden roses.   Yellow silk trousers
reached to her ankles, to her little feet in their gilded
slippers.   Her shirt of Brussa muslin, worked with silver,
revealed rounded arms, perfumed with attar of roses,
and the colour of palest amber.   Her brown hair was

arranged in eight plaits, which hung down on either side
of her on the divan. A pair of them were thick enough
to have rejoiced the heart of any fine lady in Paris. Each
braid was interwoven with threads of gold and tied at the
end with yellow ribbons, in the Armenian fashion. A
cloud of tiny, rebellious curls waved about the warm,
honey-coloured pallor of her dimpled cheeks. The amber
tones of her complexion deepened around the eyelids.
Her eyebrows, which were always close together, met that
evening in an expression of intense suffering.

Her eyes were downcast; the large, grey-green irises
veiled beneath the drooping lids. Her teeth were
clenched; her rosy lips parted in a nervous quiver,
habitual with her, and always indicating pensiveness or
pain. This little trick of hers, which would have marred
another woman's beauty, only served to enhance her
charms, and revealed two even rows of tiny, snow-white
teeth. A man would have given his soul to kiss that
quivering, crimson mouth, and those little pearls, in their
setting of ripest cherry red. I gazed with admiration at
my mistress. In this last hour I sought to steep myself
in the contemplation of her beloved features; to impress
them forever upon my mind. The strident music and the
smoke of the narghilehs gradually induced that mild
intoxication of the Orient, which brings with it the annihilation of the past and the obliteration of life's dark
hours.

A wild dream possessed my soul. Why not forget all
else, and abide with her, till the chill hour of disenchantment or death?

IX

In the midst of all that uproar, there was a tiny crash
of broken china. Aziyadé still sat motionless, but she
had crushed her cup in her convulsive grasp, and the
fragments fell to the ground. No harm was done. The
thick coffee merely left an ugly stain on her fingers, and

dripped on to the floor.   None of us seemed to have noticed the accident.

But the patch on the ground appeared to be spreading. From her clenched hand, some dark fluid kept trickling, drop by drop, then in a slender, black stream.   The room was dimly lighted by one miserable lantern.   I went close up to her.   Beside her there was a pool of blood.   The broken fragments of the cup had cut her finger to the bone.

For half an hour my darling's blood continued to flow, crimsoning basin after basin, and we could not succeed in staunching it.   We held her hand in cold water, pressing the edges of the wound together.   But nothing availed to stop the bleeding.   Pale as a girl on her deathbed, Aziyadé lay back with closed eyes.   Achmet had hurried off to rouse up an old woman, with a face like a witch, who at last contrived to staunch the blood with an application of herbs and ashes.   After advising her to keep her arm in a vertical position for the rest of the night, and extorting a fee of thirty piastres, she made some signs over the wound and went away.   Our next act was to dismiss all the dancers and put the child to bed.   She was as cold as marble, and quite unconscious.

Neither of us slept that night.   I could feel that she was suffering; her whole body was tense with pain.   The injured arm had to be held upright, as the old hag had advised, and this position gave her relief.   With my own hands I propped up her bare arm, which was burning with fever.   I could feel how each quivering fibre suddenly broke off at the edges of that deep, gaping wound.   I suffered as if it were my own flesh, not hers, that had been cut to the bone.

The moonlight fell on the bare walls and boards of our dismantled room.   The missing furniture, the rough plank tables, stripped of their silken cloths, suggested squalor, cold and desolation.   Outside the house the dogs were howling in that dismal fashion, which in Turkey, as in France, is believed to be a foreboding of death. The wind was blowing round the house, now whistling at the door, now moaning softly like an old man at the point of death. It hurt me to witness her despair; it was so deep, yet so resigned, that it would have melted a heart of stone. I was all in all to her, the only being whom she had ever loved, and who had loved her, and I was going to leave her, never to return.

"Forgive me, Loti," she said, "for cutting my hand and giving you all this trouble. I am spoiling your rest. But do go to sleep, Loti. What do my sufferings matter, as this is the end of me?"

"Listen, Aziyadé, my darling," I said. "Would you have me come back to you? . . ."

X

The next moment we were both sitting up on the edge of the bed. I was still propping up her wounded arm, and her weary head as well. Using the Mussulman formula for solemn oaths, I swore to return to her.

"Even if you are married, Loti," she said, "I shall not mind. Marry, if you like. It will not matter much. Instead of your mistress, I shall be your sister. It is your soul that I love most. Just to see you again, that is all I ask of Allah. Now I shall be almost happy; I shall live in hope. It is not quite the end of all things for Aziyadé"

After this she dropped quietly off to sleep. Dawn found her peacefully slumbering, and before sunrise I slipped away, as was my wont.

XI

I paid a hurried visit to my ship and then returned : a matter of three hours. I announced to Aziyadé a respite of two days. But two days are short enough, when they are the last in life and all that is left to two lovers, who have speedily to make the most of each other, as if they were doomed to death.

The news of my departure had already spread abroad, and I received several farewell visits from my neighbours at Stamboul. Aziyadé had shut herself up in Samuel's room and I could hear her sobbing. Something of the sound could not but reach my visitors' ears, but her presence in my house was an open secret and tacitly accepted. And only the previous evening, Achmet had publicly declared that she was Armenian. This statement, emanating from a Mussulman, was her protection.

" We always expected you to disappear like this," said the dervish Hassan-effendi, "through a trapdoor, or at the wave of a wand. Before you go, will you tell us, Arif or Loti, who you are and what you were doing here in our midst? "

Hassan-effendi was a man of honour. Much as he and his friends had desired to know who I was, they had not the remotest idea, because they had never spied upon me. The French commissary of police, who tracks you down within three hours, has not yet been introduced into Turkey. There you may still lead your own life, peaceful and unknown.

I confided to Hassan-effendi my name and status, and we promised to write to each other.

Aziyadé had been weeping for hours, but her tears were now less bitter. The prospect of seeing me again was gradually taking root in her mind and soothing her. She was beginning to say: " When you come back again. . . ."

" Yet who can tell, Loti," she mused, " if you will really come back. Allah alone knows. Every evening I shall pray *Allah! Selamet versen Loti!* (Allah, protect Loti), and then Allah will do according to his will. But, Loti," she continued mournfully, " how can I wait a whole year for you? How is it possible, when I can hardly bear a single day, a single hour, without seeing you? I never told you how, on days when you were on watch, I used to walk about on the heights of Taxim, or spend the time with my mother Behijé, because from her balcony I could gaze at the *Deerhound* in the distance. So you see, it is impossible. If you ever come back, you will find Aziyadé dead. . . ."

XII

Achmet has undertaken to send me Aziyadé's letters, and to convey mine to her through the medium of Kadija, so I must provide myself with envelopes bearing his address. Unhappily, neither Achmet nor any member of his family can write, and Aziyadé wields too bungling a pen to brave the post. So here we are, all three of us, sitting in the tent of the professional scribe; a typically Eastern vignette.

Achmet's address is extremely complicated and takes eight whole lines :

" To Achmet, son of Ibrahim, who lives at Yedi-Koule, in the cross-road that leads to Arabahdjilar-Malessi, close to the Mosque. It is the third house after a tutunji, next door to an old Armenian woman who sells drugs, with a dervish living opposite."

Aziyadé orders eight of these envelopes, for which she pays eight silver piastres of her own. In return, I have to swear to make use of them. She hides her tears in her yashmak, for this promise of mine does not reassure her. To begin with, who could expect a scrap of paper, sent all by itself from so great a distance, ever to reach her? And then she is perfectly convinced that, before long, " Aziyadé will be completely forgotten."

XIII

That evening we went by caïque up the Golden Horn. Never before had we wandered so freely all over Stamboul together in broad daylight. She seemed to disdain

all precautions, as if this were indeed the end of all things
and the world itself no longer mattered. We embarked
at the Oun-Capan jetty. Day was waning and the sun
setting in a stormy sky. Seldom in Europe do the
heavens wear so dark and angry an aspect. In the north,
the clouds were massed in that terrible arched formation
that in Africa presages a violent thunderstorm.

"Look," I said to Aziyadé, "that's just the sort of sky
I used to see every evening in the black men's country,
where I spent a year with the brother I lost."

To the south, the pointed spires of Stamboul stood out
against a great rent of flaming yellow, which shed a weird
and baleful radiance. A furious wind suddenly sprang
up on the Golden Horn. Night was falling and we were
chilled to the bone. Aziyadé's great eyes were fixed on
mine with a strangely penetrating gaze. The pupils
seemed to dilate in the gathering gloom, and to read the
very depths of my soul. I had never before seen such a
look upon her face and I felt strangely moved. It was
as if the inmost recesses of my being were bared to her,
and examined beneath the scalpel. In our last hour
together, her eyes asked of me this supreme question :

"Who are you, whom I have loved so dearly? Will
you soon forget me, like the mistress of an idle hour,
or do you really love me? Have you spoken the truth,
and will you indeed come back again?"

I have only to close my eyes to recapture that glance
of hers, to see her white-veiled head, its lines vague in
the muslin fold of the yashmak, and in the background,
that vision of Stamboul, silhouetted against the stormy
sky.

XIV

Yet once more we landed by the little square of Eyoub,
which, after to-day I should never see again. We were
anxious to take one last look together at that little home
of ours. The entrance was blocked with packing cases

and bundles, and indoors it was already dark. Achmet found an old lantern lying in a corner, which he sadly flashed around our desolate room. I was impatient to be gone, and, seizing Aziyadé by the hand, I hurried her away.

The sky was still curiously black, as if a deluge of rain were imminent. Though dark in themselves, the houses and streets seemed to stand out luminous against the murky background of the heavens. The deserted street was swept by squalls of wind, which shook every building. Two Turkish women, cowering in a doorway, looked at us inquisitively. I turned my head for one last glance at the house I was never to enter again, at that little corner of the earth, where I had known some small degree of happiness.

XV

We crossed the little square with the mosque and re-embarked. The caïque landed us at Azar-Kapou, and thence we made our way by Galata and Top-hane, to Funducli, where I had to rejoin the *Deerhound*. Aziyadé insisted on accompanying me and promised to be brave. Now that the end had come, she showed unexpected self-control. We passed through the noisy streets of Galata. This was the first time we had ever ventured together into the European quarter. " Madame " was at her door watching for us. In the young, veiled woman at my side, she found the key to the enigma, which had puzzled her for so long. Passing through Top-hane, we plunged into the deserted quarters of the Sali Bazaar, then down the broad avenues that skirt the great harems. At last we reached Funducli, where we had to bid each other farewell.

A carriage, ordered by Achmet, was waiting to take Aziyadé home.

Funducli is a little, untouched corner of old Turkey, which seems to have been transplanted from the heart of Stamboul, with its little flagged square by the sea; its ancient mosque with the golden crescent, and all round it, the tombs of dervishes and the sombre retreats of Ulema.

The storm had passed over and the sky was radiant. There was no sound, save the distant yapping of roaming dogs in the hush of the evening.

It was striking eight on board the *Deerhound*, the hour appointed for my return. I heard a whistle, which signified that one of the boats was coming for me. I could see it pulling away from the black hulk of the ship, and creeping slowly towards us. The hour was upon us, the inexorable hour of parting.

I kissed her lips and her hands, which trembled a little. Save for this, she was as calm as I myself. But she was cold as ice.

The boat came alongside the wharf. She and Achmet withdrew to a dark corner of the mosque. We pushed off, and immediately they vanished from my sight. A moment later, I heard the swift wheels of the carriage which was snatching my darling away from me forever: a sound as sinister as that of earth falling on the coffin of the beloved. All was indeed over and beyond recall. If I ever return, as I have sworn to do, the years will have shed their dust upon the past, and I myself may have set a wide gulf between us, by wedding another. She will never again be mine.

I was seized with a frantic impulse to dash after the carriage, to catch my darling to my heart, to lock my arms around her, to remain thus, she and I together, loving each other with all the force of our souls, till death should loose my clasp. . . .

XVI

March 24th.

A rainy March morning. An old Jew is removing the furniture from Arif's house, and Achmet, with a face of sorrow, is superintending the proceeding.

" Achmet, where is your master going? " ask the neighbours who were up already and standing in their doorways.

" I do not know," replies Achmet.

Damp packing cases and rain-soaked bundles are stowed away on a caïque, which sets off with them down the Golden Horn, whither, no one knows.

And that is the end of Arif. That personage has now ceased to exist. The Eastern dream is ended. The episode had such glamour, as I shall doubtless never know again; it is over, past recall, and time may sweep away its very memory.

XVII

When Achmet came on board, I told him that we had been granted a further respite of at least twenty-four hours. A storm was brewing from the direction of Marmora.

" Let us take another stroll through Stamboul," I said. " It will seem like the wanderings of disembodied spirits, not without a melancholy charm. But I am determined not to see Aziyadé again."

I went to leave my European clothes with " Madame," and once more Arif-effendi in person emerged from the tavern, and crossed the bridges, rosary in hand, with the solemn air and dignified mien, proper to all good and serious-minded Moslems, who are piously proceeding to prayer. Achmet, in his best clothes, walked beside me. He had asked me to leave the programme of our last day to him. For the moment, he was absorbed in silent grief.

XVIII

After visiting all our familiar haunts in old Stamboul, smoking a great number of narghilehs and worshipping at every mosque, we found ourselves at dusk at Eyoub.

once more, as if drawn back to that spot, where I am now no more than a homeless stranger, whose very memory will soon have passed away.

My entrance into Suleiman's café created a sensation. I was already accounted vanished and lost to sight for ever and ever. That evening there was a large mixed gathering, and I saw many new faces, which I could not place. It was almost like a mediæval resort of beggars and vagabonds.

Achmet, however, proceeded to organise a farewell celebration in my honour and sent for an orchestra, consisting of two oboes, as strident as bagpipes, a barrel organ and a big drum. I let him have his way, after exacting a solemn promise that there should be no breakages and no bloodshed. To-night we were to forget our sorrows; and I, for my part, asked nothing better. A narghileh was brought to me, together with a cup of Turkish coffee, which a child was told off to replenish every quarter of an hour. Achmet then took all the guests by the hand, formed them into a circle, and invited them to dance.

A long chain of grotesque forms began swaying backwards and forwards before my eyes, in the dim light of the lanterns. A burst of deafening music shook the rafters and wrung from the copper pans, hanging on the dark walls, metallic vibrations. The oboes shrieked and the paroxysms of devastating gaiety rose to a pitch of frenzy.

Within an hour, the whole company were intoxicated with noise and rhythmic movement. The entertainment was going with a swing. A mist rose before my eyes, and my own head was teeming with strange, incoherent thoughts. Groups of dancers, panting and exhausted, eddied hither and thither in the gloom. Still the wild whirl went on, and at each turn, Achmet broke a pane of glass with the back of his hand, till all the windows in the room were shattered, and the fragments ground to powder under the feet of the dancers. Achmet's hands were a mass of deep cuts, from which the blood poured down on to the floor. Noise and bloodshed are apparently a necessary feature of Turkish sorrow.

I was disgusted with this orgy, and anxious about Achmet's future, after witnessing this exhibition of folly, and the small regard he paid to his promises. I rose to go. Achmet understood and followed me in silence. In the cold air outside we recovered our equilibrium.

" Loti," said Achmet, " where are you going? "

" Back to the ship," I replied, " I hardly recognise you. I shall keep my promises, as you have kept yours to-night, and you will never see me again."

I walked on and began to discuss with a belated boatman the fare to Galata.

" Loti," said Achmet, " forgive me. You cannot part from your brother like this."

He burst into tears and entreaties. I had not the smallest intention of leaving him on such terms, but I felt that penance and reproof would be good for him, and I did not relent. He then caught hold of me with his bloodstained hands, and clung to me despairingly. But I pushed him roughly away and he fell against a pile of wood, which collapsed with a prodigious noise. Some bashi-bazouks on patrol, who took us for a pair of malefactors, came hurrying up with a lantern. We were on the edge of the sea, in a deserted corner of the suburb, far from the walls of Stamboul, and Achmet's gory hands looked highly suspicious.

" It's nothing," I said. " This youngster has been drinking and I am taking him home."

So I seized Achmet by the hand, and led him home to his sister Eriknaz, who first bandaged his fingers; then treated him to a long lecture, and sent him off to bed.

XIX

March 26.

One more day; one last postponement of our departure! One more day; one last change of dress at
Madame's, one last stroll through Stamboul!

The weather is lowering and sultry, the breeze warm
and mild. We spent two hours smoking our narghilehs
under the Moorish Arcades of Sultan-Sélim Street, where
white colonades, warped with age, alternate with
funerary kiosques and rows of tombs. Branches of trees,
all pink with blossom, wave above the grey walls. Green
plants are sprouting everywhere and gaily overrunning
the old sacred marble slabs. I love this country, and
delight in all these details. I love it, because it is her
own; because it is fraught with the presence of her, who
is still so near me, and whom nevertheless I must not see
again. Sunset found us seated outside the mosque of
Mehmed-Fateh, on a favourite seat, where we had whiled
away many a long hour. Scattered over the great square,
groups of Moslems were smoking and chatting, and
calmly enjoying the delights of the spring evening. The
thunderclouds had vanished and the sky was clear again.
How I have loved this spot and this Oriental life! I can
hardly believe that it is all over and that I am going away.
I gazed at the old black gateway yonder, and at the
desolate street, which dived down into a gloomy hollow.
It was there that she lived; I had only to take a step or
two to see her house again.

Achmet's eyes followed mine and he stole an uneasy
glance at me. He had read my thoughts and guessed
my purpose.

"Ah, Loti!" he cried, "if you love her, have pity on
her. You have bidden her farewell. Now leave her in
peace."

But I was determined to see her; I could not resist
my own overpowering desire. Achmet pleaded, with

tears, the cause of reason, of plain common sense.
Abeddin was there, old Abeddin her master. Any
attempt on my part to see her was sheer lunacy.

"Besides," he said, "even if she escaped from the
harem, you have no house now in which to receive her.
Where in all Stamboul, Loti, would you find hospitality
for yourself and another man's runaway wife? If she
sees you, or hears from any of the women that you are
there, she will be like a mad thing, and ruin herself. And
then to-morrow you will abandon her in the street. What
is that to you, who are going away? But if you do this,
Loti, I shall hate you. It will show that you are utterly
heartless."

Achmet hung his head and stamped his foot, his usual
procedure when my will prevailed over his. Paying no
heed to him, I went towards the portico. There I leaned
against a pillar, while my eyes scanned the street, empty
and desolate, like a street in a city of the dead. Not a
sound; not a footstep. Only the grass sprouting up
between the cobbles, and on the side walk, two dried up
carcasses of dogs.

It was an aristocratic neighbourhood. The old houses,
built of dark-hued planks, concealed unknown wealth.
All of them had shuttered balconies; shaknisirs jutting
far out into the melancholy street; iron gratings, and
behind these, dense trellises of ashwood lathing, painted
with trees and birds by artists long since dead. All the
windows in Stamboul are decorated in this fashion, and
they are always closed. In Western towns the life within
doors may be divined from without. Between the curtains, the passer-by can catch a glimpse of faces, young
or old, comely or plain. But no strange gaze can peer
into a Turkish home. If the door is unlocked to admit
a visitor, it is only half-opened, and there is always
someone behind it to close it again at once. Never a hint
betrays the privacy within.

The large house yonder, painted a dark red, is

Aziyadé's. Above the door there is a sun, a star and a crescent. Every single plank is worm-eaten. The trellis-work on the shaknisirs is adorned with blue tulips, intermingled with yellow butterflies. There is no sign of life. Yet, when you pass a Turkish house, you can never be sure whether someone is not watching you from the window.

The square on the high ground behind me was flooded with the gold of sunset. But the street lay already in shadow. Half hidden by the angle of a wall, I gazed with wildly beating heart at the house where she lived. I thought of the day when I first set eyes on her, behind the grating of her window in Salonica.

Suddenly I asked myself what I wanted and what I was doing there. I feared the mockery of Abeddin's other wives. Above all, I feared to bring about her ruin. . . .

XX

When I returned to the square of Mehmed-Fateh, the great mosque, with its Arab porticos and towering minarets, was steeped in the gold of sunset. The Ulema emerging from evening prayer were lingering on the threshold, or, with the light full upon them, standing in groups together, all the way down the great stone flight of stairs. The crowd gathered around them. In the midst of the assembly, a young man with a noble and mystic countenance was pointing towards the sky. His fine broad forehead was crowned with the white turban of the Ulema; his face was pale, while his beard and his large eyes were black as ebony. He was pointing to some invisible object up in the sky, and gazing ecstatically into the azure depths.

" Lo! there is God! " he cried. " Behold Him, ye people. I gaze upon Allah. I gaze upon the Eternal God."

Achmet and I joined in the rush towards the mystic, to whom Allah was revealed.

XXI

Alas! we could see nothing, though our need was sore. Then, as always, I would have given my life for that divine vision, my life for but one single manifestation of the supernatural.

" He lies," said Achmet, " What man has ever seen Allah?"

" Ah, it's you, Loti," exclaimed the Izzet, who was of the Ulema. " So you, too, would see Allah? Allah," he added with a smile, " does not reveal himself to infidels."

" He is mad," quoth the dervishes, and led the visionary away to the cell.

Achmet profited by this diversion to drag me away to the hill above Marmora, as far as possible from Aziyadé. By nightfall we had almost lost our bearings.

XXII

We dined under the arcades in Sultan-Selim Street. It was already late by Stamboul standards, for Turks go to bed at sundown. One by one the stars shone forth on the cloudless sky. The broad empty street, the Arab colonnades, the ancient tombs, were steeped in moonlight. Here and there a Turkish café, which was still open, cast a red glow on to the grey pavement. Passersby were few, and all of them carried lanterns. Dotted about were the dismal little lamps that burn in funerary kiosques. I looked my last at these familiar scenes. At this same hour to-morrow I should be far away.

" Let us go down to Oun-Capan," said Achmet, who had again been permitted to plan our evening. " We will ride to Balat and there take a caïque to Pri-pasha, and sleep at my sister's. She is expecting us."

We lost ourselves on the way to Oun-Capan, and all the dogs woke up and barked at us. We knew our Stamboul well, but even the old Turks go astray, at night, in these intricate mazes. There was no one to direct us. We were caught in a network of little streets, all exactly alike, straggling uphill and downhill, twisting and turning for no apparent reason, like the windings of a labyrinth. At Oun-Capan, on the outskirts of Phanar, we found two horses waiting for us, and a man to run on ahead, carrying a lantern on a six-foot pole. Away we went like the wind.

Phanar, gloomy, interminable Phanar, lay lapped in slumber. All was still. The noonday sun can hardly penetrate to these streets, where there was barely room for our two horses to keep abreast. We were hemmed in between the great wall of Stamboul on the one hand and tall buildings on the other, houses older than Islam, braced with iron, their upper storeys jutting out till they overarched these damp, narrow alleys. Riding beneath the balconies of these Byzantine mansions, we had to stoop to avoid the massive stone corbels projecting above our heads.

This was the road we always took when returning to Eyoub in the evening. At Balat, we were not very far from our own house, which was now, alas, only a thing of the past. We roused a boatman, and ferried across in his caïque to the opposite bank.

We were now in the open country. Great black cypresses towered above the plane trees. By the light of our lanterns, we scrambled up the paths that led to Eriknaz' house.

XXIII

Eriknaz-hanum was of a prepossessing and well-bred homeliness. Her complexion had a waxen pallor; while her eyes and eyebrows were black as a raven's wing. She received us unveiled, like a Frankish woman. Her whole

house suggested comfort, orderliness and exquisite clean-
liness. When we arrived, two friends of hers, Murrah
and Fenzilé, who were sitting up with her, resumed their
veils and beat a hasty retreat. They had been working
gold spangles into some of those little red slippers that
look like conchshells with their turned-up tips.

My small friend Alemshah, Eriknaz' daughter,
Achmet's niece, curled herself up on my knee, as usual,
and went off to sleep. She was a pretty little creature of
three, with great jet-black eyes, and as neat and dainty
as a doll.

After we had had a cup of coffee and a cigarette, two
mattresses, two yatags, and two coverlets were brought
in, all of them white as driven snow. After bidding us
good-night, Eriknaz retired with Alemshah, and soon
Achmet and I were fast asleep.

It was broad daylight when we were awakened by a
brilliant sun. We scrambled helter-skelter down the
paths to the Golden Horn, where a caïque was already
waiting for us. The countless black houses of Pri-pasha,
massed together in the shape of a pyramid, lay steeped in
orange light, which glittered on every window. From
the roof of their house, Eriknaz and Alemshah, their red
gowns glowing in the sunrise, watched our departure.
We passed by Eyoub, Suleiman's café, the little square
with the mosque, and the house of Arif-effendi, with the
radiance of morning full upon it. There was nobody
down by the water. Everyone was still asleep behind
locked doors. My last impression of my house, which
I had so often seen dreary and forlorn beneath the
snow, with the north wind howling round it, was one
of dazzling sunshine. My last dawn in Stamboul broke
with unusual splendour. All along the Golden Horn,
from Eyoub to Seraglio, domes and minarets stood out
against the limpid sky in all the tints of the rainbow
and the rose. Hundreds of gilded caïques, with their
freight of picturesque men and white-veiled women, went

gliding by. In less than an hour we were on board my
ship. Everything was at sixes and sevens. This time it
was no false alarm. We were to sail at noon.

XXIV

" Come, Loti," said Achmet, " let us go back to Stamboul and smoke one last narghileh together."

We raced through Sali-Bazaar, Top-hane and Galata
till we came to the Stamboul bridge. The sun was
blazing down on crowded streets. Spring had come to
stay, timing its arrival by my own departure. The
radiance of noon was streaming down on all that com-
posite mass of walls, domes and minarets, crowning the
heights of Stamboul. The light danced upon a motley
throng, arrayed in all the brightest colours of the rainbow. Strolling pedlars were shouting at the tops of their
voices, as they elbowed their way through the crowd.
Boats came and went, packed with picturesque travellers.
We knew every one of these boats, and had explored in
them every corner of the Bosphorus. We knew every
booth on the Stamboul bridge, every passer-by, every
single beggar—the whole crew of halt and blind and
maimed, of men with harelips, and men without legs. All
the riff-raff of Turkey were out of doors that morning. I
distributed alms to one and all, and reaped a perfect litany
of benedictions and salaams.

In Stamboul, we lingered awhile in the great square
of Jeni-jami, outside the mosque. For the last time in
my life, I was to taste the pleasure of sitting in Turkish
guise by the side of my friend Achmet, and smoking a
narghileh in that Oriental setting. Spring was holding
festival, with a riot of colour and gay raiment.

The whole population was out of doors, sitting under
the plane-trees, round the marble fountains, and under
the vine-clad arbours, soon to be fledged with tender
green. The barbers had brought their implements into

the street and were plying their razors in the open air.
Pious Moslems were solemnly having their heads shaved,
preserving on the very top the lock by which Mahomet
will seize them and hale them to Paradise.

But what Paradise is there for me, and who will bear
me thither, out of this old world of which I am so sick
and weary? Ah, for some Elysium where nothing will
ever change again, where I shall not be everlastingly torn
from whatever I love, from whatever loves me. If only
someone would inspire me with the Mussulman faith,
with what tears of joy should I rush to salute the green
banner of the Prophet.

XXV

"Loti," said Achmet, "Give me some idea of your
voyage."

"Achmet," I answered, "after crossing the sea of
Marmora, Ak-Deniz (the old sea), as you call it, I cross
another far bigger sea till I come to the country of the
Greeks, then a bigger one still, till I reach the country
of the Italians, which is your Madame's native land, and
after that a still bigger one, till I round the southern tip
of Spain. If I could only remain in these deep blue
waters of the Mediterranean, I should not be so very far
from you. I should have almost the self-same sky above
me, and the ships that ply to the Levant would often
bring me news from Turkey.

"But I come to yet another ocean, which is so vast
that you can form no idea of its huge expanse. And then
I sail north for several days, till I reach my own country
—a land where we have more rain than shine, more cloud
than sun. From there it is a far cry to Stamboul, and
my country bears no resemblance to yours. Everything
is paler and all the colours dimmer, just like Stamboul in
a mist, but over there the atmosphere is even less transparent than here. You have never seen such flat country,

except perhaps when you went to Arabia on your pilgrimage to Mecca, to the tomb of the Prophet. But instead of sand, there are stretches of green grass and broad acres of ploughed land. All the houses are square and exactly alike. The only prospect is one's neighbour's blank wall, and at times this flatness becomes so oppressive that one longs to climb up somewhere to obtain a wider view. But there are no steps leading up to the roof, as in Turkey, and once when I took it into my head to stroll about on my housetop, the whole neighbourhood thought I was crazy. Everyone wears a uniform dress, a grey overcoat, and a hat or a cap,—worse than at Pera. Everything is mapped out, ordered, and regulated. There are laws about everything and rules for everybody, so that the meanest lout, your hatter, or your barber, has exactly the same right as an intelligent, resolute fellow, such as you or I.

"Would you believe it, my dear Achmet, if we did a quarter of what we do daily here in Stamboul, we should be let in for an hour's argument with the police."

Achmet fully appreciated this bird's-eye view of Western civilisation and thought for a moment.

"After the war, Loti," he asked, "Why don't you bring your family to Asiatic Turkey?"

.   .   .   .

"Loti," said Achmet, "I want you to take this rosary, which I had from my father Ibrahim, and to promise never to part with it. I am quite sure," he continued, bursting into tears, "that I shall never see you again. Within a month we shall be at war. That will be the end of the unhappy Turks, and the end of Stamboul too. The Muscovites will destroy us all, and when you come back, Loti, your Achmet will be no more. His body will be lying on some northern battlefield. He will not even have a little grey marble tomb beneath the cypresses in the cemetery of Kassim-Pasha. Aziyadé will be away in Asia Minor; you will find no trace of her again. And there will be no one left to tell you of her, Loti," he sobbed. " Stay with your brother."

Alas! I dread the Muscovites no less than he. I shudder at the horrible thought that I may indeed lose all trace of her, and that no one may be left to tell me of her. . . .

XXVI

The muezzins were ascending the minarets. The hour of the midday *namaz* was at hand. It was time to go. On my way through Galata, I stopped to bid " Madame " farewell. I could have found it in my heart to embrace the old harridan. Achmet accompanied me back to the ship. There we took leave of each other, in all the confusion of inspections and preparations for getting under way.

XXVII

At Sea, March 27, 1877.

The wan March sun is sinking into the waters of Marmora. The air from the open sea blows keen and chill. The bare, desolate shores are fading into the mists of evening. Is this the end, my God? Shall I never see her again?

Stamboul is lost to sight. The loftiest domes above its tallest mosques have vanished in the distance. Everything is blotted out. I would give my life to see her for an instant and touch her hand. I am seized with a wild longing for her presence.

My head is still whirling with the clamour of the East, the crowds in the streets of Constantinople, and the stress and turmoil of departure. The stillness of the sea troubles my nerves. I cannot weep. But if only she were here I could find relief in tears. I should lay my head in her lap and cry like a child. She would see my tears and be comforted. I was stoically cold and calm when I bade her farewell, and yet I worship her. Setting aside all passion, I love her with the tenderest and purest affection. I love her heart and soul, and both are mine. I shall love her when youth has fled, when the charm of the senses has waned, in the mysterious future, which brings with it old age and death.

My heart is wrung by the sight of this calm sea and this pale sky of March. God knows my anguish! It is as if I had seen her die. I kiss every memento of her. If only I could weep! But even this relief is denied me.

At this hour she is within her master's harem, my beloved, in some room of that dreary, prison-like house, lying there, exhausted, incapable of speech or of tears, and the night is closing in upon her.

Achmet remained seated on the Funducli quay, following us with his eyes. I lost sight of him altogether with that familiar corner of Constantinople, where every evening I found either him or Samuel waiting for me.

Achmet, too, is convinced that I shall never come back. Poor little fellow; for him, too, I had a great affection. His friendship was a solace and a blessing.

I have said farewell to the East. The dream is over. My native land opens its arms to me. In peaceful little Brightbury, a warm welcome awaits me from dear ones, whose love I return.

Yet for all that it is dreary enough, that home of mine. I picture to myself that cradle of my childhood, which is still dear to me. I see the venerable, ivy-covered walls, beneath the grey Yorkshire skies; the moss-grown roofs; the lime trees, silent witnesses, in days gone by, of my earliest dreams and of the happiness that no power on earth can ever restore to me. Many a time have I come home with bleeding, aching heart. Many a time have I returned, thrilling with passions and hopes, which have always been blighted. The place is full of poignant memories. But its holy calm no longer soothes me. I feel that I shall stifle there, like a plant deprived of the sun.

XXVIII

To Loti from his Sister.

———

Brightbury, April 1877.

My dear Brother,

I, too, must write to welcome you home to England.
May He in Whom I trust, bless your return, and may
our affection serve to lighten your sorrows.   For our
part we shall leave no stone unturned to do our utmost
to help you. We are overjoyed to have you back again.

I often think, that when someone is so tenderly loved
and cherished, and comes first in the thoughts and affec-
tions of many hearts, he is hardly justified in believing
himself an outcast with a curse upon him.   I sent you a
long letter to Constantinople, which probably never
reached you.   In it I told you how deeply I entered into
your troubles and your sufferings.   Why, more than once
I have found myself shedding tears over Aziyadé's story.

Perhaps it is not altogether your fault, my little
brother, if, wherever you go, you leave a part of your
poor self behind.   Short as it is, there have been so many
conflicting claims upon your life.   But you know, I am
convinced that soon someone will take entire possession
of you, and that will do you all the good in the world.

Nightingale and cuckoo, warbler and swallow, are
here to welcome you.   You could not have chosen a better
time for your home-coming.   Perhaps we may contrive
to keep you for a little while, so as to spoil you to our
hearts' content.

Good-bye—but not for long.

Many kisses from us all.

XXIX

Translation of a rigmarole in Turkish, written to Achmet's dictation by a professional scribe, in the square of Emin-Ounou, in Stamboul, and addressed to Loti in Brightbury.

———————

" In the Name of Allah!

My dear Loti,

Achmet salutes you.

Your letter from Mitylene I sent to Aziyadé through old Kadija. Aziyadé keeps it hidden away in her gown, and has not yet had it read to her, because she has never left the house since your departure. Old Abeddin's suspicions were aroused, and he has guessed the whole story. We threw prudence to the winds those last few days. He has neither reproached her, says Kadija, nor turned her out, because he was so fond of her. But he never enters her room, and he neither speaks to her, nor takes any notice of her. The other wives, too, give her the cold shoulder, with the exception of Fenzilé-hanum, who has been to consult the *hoja* (sorcerer) on her behalf.

She has been ill ever since you left. But the big hakim (doctor) who was called in to see her, says that there is nothing the matter with her, and he has not paid a second visit. That old hag, who staunched her wounded hand, is tending her. She is in her confidence, but my own belief is that she was bribed to betray her.

Aziyadé bids me say that she has no life without you. She cannot believe that you will ever return to Constantinople; or that she will ever look into your eyes again. For her the sun seems to have gone out.

Loti, do not forget those words you said to me; never forget the promises you made me. Do you really imagine that I can know one happy moment in Constantinople

without you? No, it is impossible. When you went
away, it broke my heart with grief.

I have not yet been called up for service because of
my father, who is very old. But I expect the summons
before very long.

Your brother Achmet
salutes you.

P.S.—A fire broke out in Phanar last week, and the
whole quarter was burnt to the ground.

XXX

Loti to Izeddin-Ali at Stamboul.

Brightbury, May 20, 1877.

My dear Izeddin-Ali,

Here am I in my own country, a very different place
from yours ! I am sitting under the same old lime trees
that shaded me as a child, in that little town of Brightbury, which I described to you in Stamboul, set in the
midst of woods of green oak. Spring is here, but it
is a colourless spring, all rain and mist, rather like your
winter.

I have resumed western dress, hat and grey overcoat;
but sometimes I feel that yours is my proper dress, and
that it is only now that I am really in disguise. Yet I
am very fond of this little corner of my native land; and
of the family hearth, which I have so often deserted.
I am surrounded by those whom I love and who love me;
those, whose affection made my childhood happy and
serene. I love my surroundings, these old woods, this
countryside, which has its own peculiar charm, the deep,
pastoral charm of rural England, which I can hardly
convey to you, the charm of the past, the charm of olden
days, the charm of shepherd life of yore.

We are kept well posted, my dear Effendi, in news of the war. Things are moving rapidly. I once hoped that England would espouse the cause of Turkey. I feel only half alive, all this long way from Stamboul. You have my warmest sympathy. I love your country and I offer my sincere prayers for your success. I think you will soon see me back again.

You must have guessed, Effendi, my love for her, whose presence in my house you divined and condoned. You have a generous heart; you rise superior to all conventions and prejudices. Surely then I may tell you that I love her, and that it is for her sake, above all, that I shall soon return.

XXXI

Brightbury, May, 1877.

I was sitting under the old lime trees at Brightbury. Above my head a blue-tit was pouring out its little soul in a long and complicated melody. Its singing stirred in me a world of memories. At first it was all confused, like glimpses of a distant past. But gradually the visions took shape, and grew clearer and more precise, until it all came back to me.

It was over there in Stamboul. We were engaged on one of our rashest ventures, one of our days of reckless truancy. But Stamboul was so big, we argued, nobody knew us, and old Abeddin was away in Adrianople.

It was a bright winter afternoon and we were out wandering together, she and I, rejoicing like a couple of children to be out in the sun for once, and roaming the countryside. But we had chosen a cheerless region for our walk. We were strolling along by the great wall of Stamboul, the most solitary spot in the world, where nothing seems to have stirred, since the days of the last Byzantine Emperors. This great city's means of communications are all by sea. The ancient ramparts are steeped in a silence, such as broods over the approach to a necropolis. Here and there a gate has been built in the thickness of these walls, but to no purpose, for never a soul goes in or out. These queer, little, low doors have an air of mystery, and above the lintels are gilded inscriptions and curious decorations. Between the inhabited quarters of the town and the fortifications, lie great tracts of waste land, dotted with suspicious-looking hovels, and with crumbling ruins, dating from every epoch of history. There is nothing from without to break the eternal monotony of these walls, save here and there the white shaft of a minaret, rising in the distance. Always the same battlements, the same turrets, the same dark hues, laid on by the hand of time, the same regular lines, running straight and dreary, till they are lost on the far horizon.

We were walking all alone at the base of these great walls. The surrounding country was studded with clumps of towering cypresses, as tall as cathedrals, beneath whose shade thousands of Osman sepulchres lay crowded together. In no other country have I seen so many cemeteries, so many tombs, so many dead.

" This," said Aziyadé, " is a favourite haunt of Azrael. He alights here at night, folds his great wings, and wanders in human shape beneath these fearsome shades."

It was very still in this realm of the dead, in these solemn, awe-inspiring groves. But we two were enjoying the adventure, glad to be young, and, for once, roaming together in the open air, under the clear blue sky, like ordinary mortals.

She had pulled her thick yashmak over her forehead as far as her eyes. Her veil was drawn so close that I could hardly see her flashing orbs, so limpid and so mobile. Her borrowed ferenje was of sober cut and colour, such as was seldom worn by fastidious young women. Old Abeddin himself would not have recognised her.

We walked with swift elastic step over the little white daisies and the short grass of January, filling our lungs with the keen, bracing air of that glorious winter day.

Suddenly, through the deep silence, we heard a tit singing deliciously, just like that tit to-day. Birds of the same species repeat the identical song in every corner of the world. Aziyadé stood still in amazement. With a comical air of surprise, she pointed her henna-stained finger at the tiny songster, perched on a cypress branch close by. The little fellow, so small and solitary, was expending so much energy and posturing with such a merry, swaggering air, that we both laughed for joy. We stood listening to him for a long time, till he was frightened away by six big camels, roped one behind the other, which came lumbering towards him.

Afterwards . . . afterwards . . . we saw moving in our direction a group of women dressed in mourning, who proved to be Greeks. Two Greek priests were walking at the head of the little procession, and the women were carrying a tiny corpse, which lay with uncovered face on a bier, according to custom.

" *Bir gujel tchoudjouk!* (What a sweet little creature !)," said Aziyadé suddenly serious.

The dead child was a pretty little girl of four or five, like an exquisite wax doll; she lay on her pillows, as if asleep, dressed in a dainty frock of white muslin with a wreath of gilded flowers upon her head.

A grave had been dug at the side of the road, for the Greeks bury their dead no matter where, by the highway, or at the foot of the city walls.

" Let us join them," said Aziyadé, a child again, " they will give us some sweets."

In order to dig the grave, it had been necessary to oust a previous occupant, who could not have been buried long, for the surrounding earth was full of bones and bits of tattered cloth. The chief relic was an arm bent in a right angle, the bones still red, and held together at

the elbow by some ligament which the earth had not
devoured.

The two officiating popes, who had long hair like
women, were a pair of unwashed gallowsbirds, arrayed
in dirty finery, and had four rascally choirboys for
assistants.   They gabbled some words over the little
body; then the mother removed the wreath of flowers,
and drew a nightcap over the small head, tucking away
the golden curls, with a preciseness that would have made
us smile, had it not been the act of a bereaved mother.

When the child had been laid in the grave, on the bare
damp soil, with neither planking nor bier beneath her,
all that foul earth was shovelled over her.   Everything,
including the old elbow bone, was thrown back into the
pit, covering the dear little waxen face.   She was soon
completely buried and out of sight.

We were given some sweets, as Aziyadé had foreseen
—a Greek custom unknown to me.   A girl with a bag
of white sugar-almonds doled out a handful to each by-
stander, including ourselves, although we were apparently
Turks.   Aziyadé put out her hand for her share, and her
eyes filled with tears.

XXXII

It was odd, was it not, of that little bird to be so full
of the joy of life, so gay, in those funereal surroundings?

V

I

May 20th, 1877.

Who could mistake the clear blue sky, the azure sea of the Levant? What is that yonder, dawning in the distance? Mosques and minarets stand out on the horizon. With beating heart I behold Stamboul once more. I land, conscious of deep emotion on finding myself in this country again.

But now there was no Achmet at his post, curvetting on his white horse at Top-Hané. Galata, once so busy, was still as death. It was clear that some terrible ordeal, such as a war of extermination, was proceeding far from the city's precincts.

I resumed my Turkish dress, and hastened away to Azar-Kapou. There I took the first caïque I saw and was recognised by the caïqji.

" What of Achmet? " I asked.

" Gone. Gone to the war."

I called on his sister, Eriknaz.

" Yes, he has gone," she told me. " He was at Batum. But we have had no news of him since the battle."

Her dark eyebrows were drawn together with pain. She was shedding bitter tears for the brother, of whom men had bereft her, and little Alemshah wept, too, as she looked at her mother.

I went to Kadija's house, but the old beldame had moved, and no one could tell me where she was living now.

177

II

All alone, I made my way to the mosque of Mehmed-Fateh, which was close to Aziyadé's house. There were no ideas in my troubled mind; nor had I any plan of action. I was actuated solely by my yearning to be near her and to see her again.

I traversed the heap of ruins and ashes, which was all that remained of wealthy Phanar, one vast scene of desolation, an endless succession of devastated streets, littered with charred and blackened wreckage. This was the same Phanar, through which I would ride so gaily of an evening, on my way to Eyoub, where my love awaited me.

Shouts rang out in these desolate streets. Levies for the war, half savage, half clothed, and scantily armed, were standing about in groups, sharpening their yataghans on the stones and flourishing old green banners with inscriptions in white lettering.

I walked on and on, passing through the deserted quarters of Eski-Stamboul. I drew nearer and nearer, till at last I entered the gloomy street, which slopes up to Mehmed-Fateh, the street in which she lived. The sun beat down on a scene so forbidding that my heart sank. There was not a soul to be seen in that melancholy street; nothing broke the intense silence, save my own footsteps. Then, creeping over the cobbles and the green grass, close to the wall, came the form of an old woman. Lean, bare legs of ebony black showed beneath the folds of her cloak. She pattered along with her head down, muttering to herself. . . . It was Kadija.

Kadija recognised me.

" Ah ! " she exclaimed with a sneer. Her voice had that indescribable shrillness common alike to monkeys and negresses.

" Aziyadé ? " I asked.

" *Eulu! Eulu!* " she replied, purposely dwelling on

these weird and barbaric syllables, which in Tartar signified death.

"*Eulu! eûlmûch!*" she persisted, as if addressing someone who could not understand. With a leer, in which hatred was mingled with a grim satisfaction, she ruthlessly pursued me with that baleful utterance:

"Dead! Dead! She is dead."

The mind cannot grasp at once words such as these, that fall like a bolt from the blue. It takes a moment for grief to pounce, and fasten its fangs in the heart of its victim. Aghast at my own calmness, I walked on, with the old crone following me like a fury, step by step, uttering her horrible cry of "*Eulu! Eulu!*" Behind me I could feel the burning hatred of this old creature who had worshipped her mistress, for whose death she held me responsible. I dared not turn to look at her, I dared not question her, lest proof should bring conviction. I walked on and on, like a drunken man.

III

When I came to myself, I was leaning against a marble fountain, near the house with the blue tulips and yellow butterflies, where Aziyadé used to live. I was sitting on the ground and my head was swimming. The dark, desolate houses were dancing a macabre dance before my eyes. My forehead had struck the marble basin and was bleeding. A gnarled, black hand, wet with cold water from the fountain, was supporting my head. Beside me, I saw Kadija, dissolved in tears. I pressed her wrinkled, monkey-like hands, and she went on bathing the cut on my brow.

A group of men passed by, but paid no heed to us. They were talking excitedly, and reading some of the leaflets, which were being distributed in the streets, with the news of the first battle of Kars. It was in the first dark days when the fate of Islam seemed already sealed.

IV

" All night, all day, I wake. My fevered brow
Is racked with dreams. My hot tears never cease,
Since my Albaydé closed her fawnlike eyes
In Death's eternal peace."

(—VICTOR HUGO. *Oriental Poems.*)

This cold, hard thing, which I was clasping was a
marble stele, planted upright in the ground. It was
painted azure blue, and carved at the top with a bas-relief
of gilded flowers. I can still see those flowers, and the
bold, gilt lettering, which my eyes read mechanically. . . .
It was one of those monumental stones, which in Turkey
are dedicated only to women. I was seated on the ground
in the great cemetery of Kassim-Pasha, beside a mound
of newly-turned earth, the length of a human form. The
loose soil was strewn with tiny plants, dislodged by the
spade, and lying with their roots in the air. Round the
grave there were moss, smooth turf and fragrant wild
flowers. No bouquets or wreaths are ever laid on
Turkish tombs.

This cemetery had none of the horror that invests our
European burial-grounds. Oriental melancholy of a
milder yet sublimer quality pervaded its great stretches
of mournful solitude, its barren hills, dotted with dark
cypresses. Here and there, in the shade of these mighty
trees, lay newly cut sods, ancient steles, tombstones, and
curious Turkish sepulchres, surmounted with tarbooshes
and turbans. Far away, at my feet, stretched the Golden
Horn, the familiar outlines of Stamboul, and yonder . . .
Eyoub.

It was a summer evening. The earth, the dry grass,
everything felt warm to the touch, except that marble
stele which I was clasping. It was never anything but
cold, for it had its base imbedded in the ground, and was
continually chilled by its contact with the dead.

Surrounding objects took on the strange aspect, which

external things assume, when the destinies of men and empires have reached some great decisive crisis; when fulfilment is at hand.

The troops were setting out for the Holy War. From afar I heard their clarions; sounding in strident, sonorous unison. There is a weirdness in those Turkish clarion-calls; they have a tone which you will not hear on our Western bugles.

Hallali! they seemed to cry. Sound the Mort! Islam and the Orient are driven to bay, and the great race of Chengiz is dying, dying, dying.

I had a Turkish yataghan in my sword-belt. I was in the uniform of a *yuzbashi;* no longer was I Loti. I was now Arif, Arif-Ussam, *yuzbashi.* I had begged to be sent to the front, and I was leaving on the following day.

A vast and brooding melancholy hovered over this consecrated ground of Islam. The setting sun gilded the weather-stained marble tombstones; its rays touched the great cypresses, illuminating the immemorial trunks, the dark and gloomy branches. The cemetery was like a titanic temple of Allah. It had a temple's mystic tranquillity, and, like a temple, it bade one kneel and pray.

I gazed on it as through a funeral veil. The events of my past life whirled through my head in the crazy disorder of a dream. I saw the corners of the world in which I had lived, and loved. I saw my friends, my brothers, the mistresses I had adored in the East and in the West, and, then alas! I saw the well-loved home I had forever deserted, the leafy lime-trees, and my mother. . . .

All had been forsaken for the sake of her who lay within that tomb. She had worshipped me with the deepest, the purest, the humblest love.

Slowly and softly, behind the gilded bars of the harem, she had died of grief, though no word of complaint had ever reached me. I can still hear her saying, with gentle seriousness :

"You know, I am only a little Circassian slave. Whereas you, oh, you understand! Leave me, Loti, if you will. You must do what seems best to you."

The clarion-calls, sounding from afar, rang out like the trumps of doom. Thousands of men shouted with one accord the terrible name of Allah. The distant clamour reached me where I was standing, and filled the vast cemeteries with a strange confusion of sounds.

The sun had now sunk behind the holy hill of Eyoub. The heritage of Othman lay before me in the clearness of a summer night.

That sinister thing that lies there under the soil, so near me that I shudder at the thought of it—that sinister thing, already consumed by the earth—I love it still. Oh, God in Heaven, is this all? Or is there not, in truth, an impalpable something, a soul, hovering near me in the pure evening air, a soul that can still see me as I stand here, earthbound and weeping?

Her memory almost persuades me to prayer. My heart, hardened and shrunken in the farce of life, now lies open to all the exquisite delusions of faith. My tears fall without bitterness on the naked earth. If soul and body end not in dark dust, perchance I shall soon know. I can at least seek death, so that this knowledge may be mine.

V

CONCLUSION

The following announcement appears in the Djeridei-Havadis, a Stamboul newspaper:

The body of a young English naval officer, who recently enlisted in the Turkish army under the name of Arif-Ussam, has been found among those who were killed in the last battle of Kars.

The body has been interred at the foot of Kizil-Tépé, in the plain of Kara-Jemir, amongst the faithful defenders of Islam, which may the Prophet protect!